The Two Angels

The Two Angels

by

Richard Terrain

The Two Angels

Dedicated to Leanne, the nicest security guard this side of the planet.

The Two Angels

FADE IN:

OPENING CREDITS

A Christmas tree with glittering lights from bottom to top while a Country song plays.

Close-up on various ornaments (glass balls, bears, mooses, candy bars), following the twinkling garlands to the top where a magnificent angel towers.

END OF OPENING CREDITS:

EXT. RESIDENTIAL STREET - NIGHT

It is a clear full moon night over a residential neighborhood. A huge house heavily illuminated with Christmas decorations. The garden is covered with fake snowflakes.

A loud party music resounds from inside the house.

EXT. HOUSE - NIGHT

On the doorstep, PEOPLE smoke and drink, noisily chat and laugh. The front door opens and a couple appears.

SCOTT (30), relaxed, pleasant, informal, looks quite drunk. CHARLI (25) follows him. She is a blonde young woman

The Two Angels

with sad and aloof eyes. On the threshold, she stares at Scoot, rather worried to see him in such state.

SMOKING WOMAN Bye Scott. Bye Charli.

CHARLI See you, Trisha.

Scott chuckles and walks down the garden path. He slips on the gravel and nearly falls.

CHARLI

(to Scott)

>I'll drive. Gimme the keys.

SCOTT

(woozy)

>I'm okay, honeybunch.

CHARLI

(sharply)

You're not. You perfectly know I don't like you to drive and drink that much. Especially by night.

Scott gets nervous.

SCOTT

I said I'm okay!

Charli stops walking.

CHARLI

(firmly)

Then I'm not coming with you.

Scott turns to her, furious.

SCOTT You what?!

He grabs her arm.

SCOTT

Listen, you're my wife. Ya're going everywhere I go.

CHARLI

Scott, stop it! You're hurting me!

He releases her and grins a smile.

SCOTT

I'm sorry honeybunch. I didn't mean to. But, I'm okay. (beat)

I promise. I'll drive. (gently) Come on.

He kindly puts his finger on her nose. Charli cannot help sadly smiling.

CHARLI

(playing his game) Beep.

EXT. RESIDENTIAL STREET - NIGHT

Scott and Charli pace down the street to a white Civic. They enter the car.

INT. CAR - NIGHT

Though he has some troubles with the starting key, Scott manages to start the engine. Charli fastens her seat belt.

SCOTT

(winningly)

Relax honeybunch. I said I was sorry. Okay? (a beat)

Hey, wanna see some magic?

Charli simply smiles. Scott rummages under his seat and takes a small present out he hands to Charli.

SCOTT

Merry Christmas honeybunch.

Charli's face enlightens.

SCOTT Hope you'll like it.

Charli takes the present, unwraps it, and opens the little box sized like a jewel box to find-- --a tiny MP3 player.

SCOTT

Ya'll listen to your music anytime you'll want to now.

CHARLI

(bitterly)

Yeah, and won't bother you anymore.

Scott cannot find an answer. He just bursts out laughing and slaps his hands.

SCOTT (like a kid)

Okay. Where's mine?

CHARLI At home.

SCOTT

Why? Was it too big to be hidden in the car?

CHARLI

(wisely)

You'll see. It's a surprise.

He speeds up. Charli turns the radio on. A song plays.

SONG ON RADIO

"Daddy just loves his children every now and then, it's a love without end, amen, it's a love without end, amen--"

After a while, Charli turns to Scott.

CHARLI

Scott. Why didn't you ever talk about having a baby? Why don't we have a normal life like our friends?

As he drives and acts as if he had not heard her, Scott changes the station.

SONG ON RADIO

"Hark! The herald angels sing glory to the newborn king--"

Scott turns the radio off.

SCOTT

I'm sick of that Country music and Christmas rubbish!

Charli does not answer. From under his seat, Scott takes a bottle of whisky, uncorks it, and starts to drink.

The Two Angels

Silent, Charli stares at him with some kind of disgust.

The car speeds up in the night.

FADE TO:

INT. THOMAS' APARTEMENT - NIGHT

A small and merely decorated apartment with a tiny Christmas tree on a silent TV set. A little Christmas music plays.

By the window, a large drawing board with many pencils, ink pots, brushes, and an unfinished comics strip page.

Outside, through the window, it snows. A real Christmas night.

On the TV screen, in B&W, young Jimmy Stewart runs and happily shouts through snowy streets. O.S., a snuffling can be heard.

LINDA (O.S.) Believe me or not, but it's the most depressing and the most beautiful movie I've ever seen.

THOMAS (O.S.)

Yeah. "I wish I had a million dollars".

LINDA & THOMAS (O.S.) "Hot dog"!

THOMAS (30) is a good-looking guy-next-door kind with a little spark in the eyes. At his side, LINDA (33), a "funny girl", snuffles. They are both slouched on a small sofa and watch TV.

As Thomas wears his everyday clothes, Linda wears an elegant red lamé dress with a décolleté. She is rather sexy. Thomas eats pizza and drinks a soda.

The Two Angels

LINDA

It's a real pleasure to watch it every Christmas. Thank you for having turn your TV in black and white. I can't stand those awful colorized old movies.

Now on TV, Stewart warmly hugs his kids by a Christmas tree, surrounded by many people who sing.

Thomas starts to weep.

THOMAS

(as an excuse)

I've got something in my eye.

LINDA

(doubtful) Of course.

THOMAS

Oh Linda. What I'd give to have kids? Being married, have a big house, a dog, a life insurance, ten credits on my back and an endearing mother-in-law. A normal life.

LINDA I know what you mean. (with irony)

I have that nightmare too.

THOMAS

You know, sometimes, I do feel myself like a failure. I'm thirty, alone in life. Unable to create a proper world sale comics.

LINDA

You're not a failure Thomas. You've got a nice job and a whole life ahead.

The Two Angels

THOMAS

Then, tell me why every girl I choose manages to break my heart in millions pieces and steps on it with the most sadistic smile?

LINDA

(shrugging)

You're a softie and you haven't found the right one yet, that's why. It's not your fault. It'll come in right time.

(singing) Someday, your princess will come.

THOMAS

But Sandy was my princess. She finally was the girl of my dreams. The one I was going to cherish all my life and have a dozen kids with.

Linda bitterly grins.

LINDA

She looked rather like a witch to me. I could easily see her with a red apple in hand.

THOMAS

No, she wasn't. She was everything

I'd have wished for. Everything. Brown kinky eyes, long dark hair, that fringe over her eyes and that devastating smile that made me melt each time I was looking at her.

LINDA

The Two Angels

In your dreams, but, hey, I've got breaking news for you: girls lie too. Anyway, I didn't like her, I didn't like her manners-- (beat)

--and, most of all, I didn't like her ass.

On the TV screen, movie ends. Linda gets up and stretches.

LINDA

You're sure you'll be alright?

THOMAS

(sighing)

I don't know if I'm getting better or just used to the pain.

Linda takes her coat and wears it.

LINDA

Yes, I know that you mean. Cheer up anyway Thomas. It's a wonderful life after all. Tonight it's peace on Earth and--

THOMAS

(interrupting) Your eye's black.

Linda stands in front of a mirror and realizes her mascara has dripped.

LINDA

I'll fix that in my car. (beat)

You sure you're not coming. That's your final word?

Thomas gets up at his turn and his hand awkwardly bumps into the soda can. The soda spills on the floor.

THOMAS

Damn. I have to clean that carpet again.

LINDA

(twitting)

Leave it. That'd be rather artful by the ketchup spot.

Thomas sighs.

THOMAS

Anyway, I'll make you a promise. This is the last Christmas I'll spend alone.

LINDA

(winking)

I knew it. You're a winner after all. A bit awkward, but a winner anyway.

He takes her to the door.

THOMAS Am I? Really ?

LINDA

(serious) Just remember I love you.

THOMAS I love you too.

They hug. Thomas opens the door.

LINDA

Merry Christmas.

THOMAS

Merry Christmas Linda.

She exits and leaves Thomas by himself.

INT. CAR - NIGHT

Scott still drives and sips his whisky. Increasingly drunk, he exhilaratingly sings on "Winter Wonderland" tune in front of Charli's dark eyes.

SCOTT

(singing out loud)

Lacy things, the wife is missing, didn't ask her permission, I'm wearing her clothes, her silk pantyhose, walking 'round in women's underwear--

He laughs by himself.

CHARLI

(shaking her head)

That's definitely the last Christmas I'll spend with you.

As if he didn't listen to her, Scott lowers his window and waves to some cows.

SCOTT

(shouting)

Merry Christmas girls!! Yahoo!!! He drinks up.

INT. THOMAS' APARTEMENT - BATHROOM - NIGHT

In front of his bathroom cabinet mirror, Thomas stares at his own reflection. He raises a bottle of whisky and cheers to the mirror.

THOMAS

(to his reflection) Merry Christmas.

He chuckles with irony, drinks up and coughs, apparently not used to drink whisky. Then, he opens the cabinet door and faces small boxes of pills.

THOMAS

(to himself) Showtime.

EXT. COUNTRYSIDE ROAD - NIGHT

Scott speeds up on the road. The engine roars.

CHARLI Scott, please!

But Scott does not listen to her. He slips again his head out of the window and shouts.

INT. THOMAS' APARTEMENT - BATHROOM - NIGHT

Thomas takes a mouthful of pills and drinks to swallow them.

THOMAS

(to himself) To Chris.

He swallowers and takes another mouthful of pills and whisky.

THOMAS (cont'd)

(to himself) To Chelly.

Another mouthful of pills and whisky.

THOMAS

(to himself)

To Sandy.

The Two Angels

(nervously chuckling) Merry Christmas girls.

INT. CAR - NIGHT

His head out through the window and still shouting, Scott does not see the truck coming onto the Civic, horn blaring. Its headlights light inside the car and Charli screams. She protects her face with the hands.

INT. THOMAS' APARTEMENT - BATHROOM - NIGHT

Thomas heavily collapses on the bathroom tiled floor, dropping the pills and the bottle of whisky.

INT. CAR - NIGHT

At the very last moment, Scott enters his head into the Civic and pumps the brakes. He saws away inexpertly at the wheel and restores the direction. He manages to avoid the truck.

The car slides on the road, speeds on the side and dives onto a field to finish its course at the foot of a tree.

The windshield shatters in millions pieces.

INT. THOMAS' APARTEMENT - BATHROOM - NIGHT

His face glued on the bathroom tiled floor, Thomas slowly closes his eyes.

FADE OUT:

FADE IN:

INT. HEAVEN'S GATES - NIGHT

SLOW OPENING TO REVEAL A SHINING FOG

The Two Angels

Through the fog, a FEMALE ECHOED VOICE can be heard as coming from a loudspeaker in many languages.

FEMALE VOICE (V.O.) Ladies and gentlemen, we are glad to welcome you. You have choose the right path--

Slowly, the fog vanishes and reveals a weird place looking like a huge airport departure hall. Instead of material walls, everything is made out of the same shining fog.

FEMALE VOICE (V.O.) Please stand on line until someone will present to you. It won't take long before you will be taken in charge. Just be patient--

In front of different desks made out of the same fog, parallel lines of PEOPLE. People of all ages, all races, and all conditions.

As they slowly advance to the desks, a MAN or a WOMAN comes to them and warmly hugs them. Dressed up with long dark coats, they each wear a benevolent smile.

Each NEWCOMER is led by one of them to different escalators made out of fog.

Standing on one line, Thomas waits for his turn and seems to not understand what he does there. He just looks hypnotized by the spectacle around him like everyone else.

On a parallel line stands Charli. She still has her sad eyes. Scanning the place, her look meets Thomas. As she stares at him, she feels bizarre.

Suddenly, she puts her hand at her heart level as if it was bumping hard down inside of her. She lowers her head to her chest and smiles. Though she is far from the desk in front of her, she sees an OLD LADY coming to her.

OLD LADY

(sweet)

Would you mind coming with me my child?

She gently takes her by the hand and leads her through the hall. As they walk away, Thomas turns his head and sees Charli's back of the head.

Puzzled, Thomas waits for his turn to be taken in charge. He finally reaches the desk and a woman (ANGELA) comes to him. She is in her middle-thirties, dark-hair with a bun, and smiling.

She hugs him. Thomas' confusion is deeper.

ANGELA

My name is Angela and I'm the one who'll show you around today.

She gently takes him by the hand and they walk to one of the escalators.

THOMAS

(confused)

Where-- are we?

ANGELA

Is Heaven meant something special to you?

THOMAS

(confused) Am I-- dead?

ANGELA

(gently) Yes, you are.

THOMAS

But, I thought because--

ANGELA

(interrupting)

I know. Because you committed suicide. But Hell is just a legend. There is no Hell. There is just one place. Here. Even evil minds are welcome. Redemption is offered to everyone.

THOMAS

(chuckling) So, I'm really dead.

ANGELA

(as reciting)

You'll be through different levels, seven exactly, before you could, if you will, become an angel or being reincarnated.

Thomas interrupts her.

THOMAS

(curious)

You mean that I will be able to go back?

ANGELA

(embarrassed)

Well, yes. But not how you'd expected.

INT. HEAVEN'S GATES - ESCALATOR - NIGHT

They reach a spiral escalator made out of the same clouds and start to make their way up.

ANGELA

I'm sure you'll meet people here you knew during your existence, friends, relatives, and you'll soon be ready to welcome newcomers just like I do.

As they go up, Thomas turns back and looks down at the huge hall.

THOMAS

I can't believe it. There are so many people.

ANGELA That's the circle of life, Thomas.

THOMAS

(floored) How do you know my name?

ANGELA We know everything about you.

THOMAS

(ironically) Do you? Really?

ANGELA

Well, not me. But it's all written in the Big Book.

(beat)

You'll soon get every answer you wish.

As they keep going up, they cross a second escalator on its way down. Charli and the old lady are on it.

Charli'S EYES AND THOMAS' MEET

IT IS LOVE AT FIRST SIGHT

They cannot take their eyes off each other. A deep and intense look.

Thomas does not listen anymore to Angela. All he hears is the old lady who tells Charli.

OLD LADY

(with a slight echo) Don't worry Mrs. McKenna, you'll soon be back in Baton-Rouge as if nothing had happened.

As Charli goes down and Thomas goes up, they keep exchanging looks. Thomas can see some kind of despair in Charli's eyes as she gets slowly away.

While Angela keeps on talking, Thomas turns to her and interrupts her.

THOMAS What's that escalator?

ANGELA

(mindless)

Oh, that one? It's exclusively for people who weren't supposed to die. It simply wasn't their time. It's their way down back to Earth.

Thomas turns a last time to Charli. She grins a little helpless smile and mouths "Thank you" to him. Thomas can see regrets in her eyes as she slightly waves to him before she disappears into the shining fog.

ANGELA We'll soon be arrived. (with a smile)

Even here we have administrative tasks to fill.

They finally reach the top of the escalator.

INT. HEAVEN'S GATES - OFFICES - NIGHT

The entire floor is made of glass wall offices. In each office, a NEWCOMER is seated in front of THREE CLERKS and, apparently, answers questions.

ANGELA

Your soul is gonna be weighted and judged. A good point for each virtue, a bad for every sin.

At the end of one couloir, a shout. A MAN, at the verge of the nervous breakdown, furiously struggles.

THE MAN

(shouting)

I don't want to be dead! There should be a mistake! My wife and my son need me!

Several angels try to calm him down, but the man keeps on violently struggling.

AN ANGEL

(shouting)

Help! We need help!

Angela turns to Thomas.

ANGELA

I'll be right back.

She rapidly paces to help her colleagues and leaves Thomas by himself. He watches her rushing away for a short while, and then turns back. The way to the "Escalator to Earth" is safe.

NO ONE IN SIGHT

Slowly, step after step, Thomas walks back and gets close to the steps. As he approaches, the escalator automatically moves down.

INT. HEAVEN'S GATES - EARTH ESCALATOR - NIGHT

Thomas starts to go down, trying to act naturally. On his way down, he crosses NEWCOMERS and ANGELS on the spiral escalator on their way up.

But the angels are too busy to explain the newcomers that they hardly notice him.

A VOICE RESOUNDS BEHIND HIM

VOICE (O.S.)

Hey you! Where do you think you're going!!

Thomas turns back and realizes that an ANGEL MAN calls him. Thomas starts to rush down the stairs and do not look back anymore.

ANGEL MAN (O.S.) Come back here! You're not allowed to go down! Stop!

Thomas now runs down for a long descent through the shining fog. Suddenly, as if there was no more stairs under his feet, he slips and disappears into a deep black hole.

EXT. SKIES - NIGHT

Thomas falls through a black sky, through clouds, when he sees the earth getting closer and closer as if he was jumping with a parachute.

A LONG, LONG, AND UNREAL FALL

The Two Angels

His face is distorted by the incredible fall speed. Now, he can rapidly discern city lights, a city, house blocks, a building, a roof--

He closes his eyes at the moment he is about to crash on the roof.

FADE OUT:

FADE IN:

INT. HOSPITAL ROOM - NIGHT

A SLIGHT BEEP RESOUNDS

CLOSE-UP OF Charli'S OPENING EYES

Charli realizes she's laid in a hospital bed. The room is dimly lighted with a small bedside lamp. Two transparent tubes are connected to her nose and an IV drip is attached to her arm. She looks weak and seems to be sleeping quietly, breathing in rhythm of an ECG monitor at her side.

Charli hardly moves her head. Her eyes scan the room. She notices that Scott is seated by the bed, dozing. He has bruises and a bandage around his head.

Charli slowly moves her arm and her hand meets a steel tray on the table side. The tray falls on the plastic floor in a metallic crash.

The noise wakes Scott in a jump. When he realizes that Charli is waking, he rushes to the bedroom door, and shouts into the hallway.

SCOTT

(shouting)

Nurse! She's waking up!!

Scott comes back to the bed. He kneels by Charli, happy, and kisses her hand.

SCOTT

Oh, honeybunch. You're back! You're back!

He starts to sob. A NURSE enters. When she sees Charli, she immediately steps out and call.

NURSE (O.S.)

Doctor Grant! Doctor Grant!

SCOTT

(sobbing)

Honeybunch. I'll never leave you anymore! I've been so stupid!

He kisses her hand.

SCOTT

I love you so. When I think I could've lose you! Say something! Speak to me!

CHARLI

(hardly)

Scott--

SCOTT Yes!

The nurse comes back with DOCTOR GRANT who leans over Charli and gently pushes Scott back.

DOCTOR GRANT

The Two Angels

Mrs. McKenna, welcome back. I could say I had a hard poker game with the Bearded One above. Well.

Apparently, I won. (sigh)

But let me tell you, you can consider yourself as a miraculously healed after one night of deep coma. I've never saw that. An incredible recovery. The good news is I think that you'll both be able to get out on tomorrow after an overnight on observation.

Charli hardly nods.

DOCTOR GRANT

(to Scott)

Take good care of your wife. She came back for you.

SCOTT Yes Doctor.

Doctor Grant and the nurse step out. Scott kneels again by Charli and takes her hand.

SCOTT

He's right. You're back for me honeybunch. It's now time for us to have a baby. A beautiful baby from you. A lovely baby with his mother's eyes. (beat)

What do you think?

Charli does not answer.

SCOTT

Tell me. What about Nicholas for a boy? Or Emma for a girl? Or Sandra? Or Calvin? Or--

Charli puts her hand on his.

The Two Angels

CHARLI

(interrupting him) We'll see later.

SCOTT No problem. You'll choose.

He puts his finger on her nose. This time, Charli turns her head away.

CHARLI

Scott. I'm so tired.

She closes her eyes.

FADE OUT:

FADE IN:

INT. THOMAS' APARTEMENT - BATHROOM - DAY

BLACKNESS

A commercial for Christmas bargain can be heard from a TV O.S..

CLOSE-UP OF THOMAS' OPENING EYE

He is laid on the bathroom tiled floor, amid the pills, by the empty bottle of whisky. Some pills are even glued on his cheek.

As he moves, Thomas puts his hand on the forehead and grins with pain. He hardly stands up, woozy and reclines against the bathroom wall. As he tries to recover, he sweeps the pills off his cheek and sighs.

INT. THOMAS' APARTEMENT - DAY

Thomas clumsily steps to the couch and lets himself heavily slouch in it. His hand reaches for the remote and he turns the TV off.

THOMAS

(to himself)

What a nightmare.

Someone knocks on his door. At first, Thomas does not move, but the knock resounds again and Linda's voice can be heard from behind the door.

LINDA (V.O.) Thomas! It's me! Open, please!

Thomas gets up, walks to the door, takes a look in the peephole, and opens. Linda enters like a fury.

LINDA

Where the hell have you been? I came yesterday and you weren't home. I started to worry. You even didn't answer the phone.

THOMAS

(woozy) I'm okay.

LINDA

You're okay?! Have you seen yourself? You really look like shit.

Thomas holds his forehead and closes back the door.

THOMAS

(grimacing) Please, don't shout.

LINDA

Don't tell me you've got a hangover?

THOMAS

(nodding) I have.

He steps back to the couch and sits down, but he misses it to find himself butt on the floor.

LINDA

Welcome at last to the adult world.

She leans over him and notices a pill by his ear.

LINDA

I don't believe it.

She goes directly to the bathroom, takes a glimpse and comes back.

LINDA

Don't tell me you did--?

THOMAS

(sighing)

Do you realize that I've even failed that? Even up there, they didn't want me.

LINDA

Luckily, you failed. Are you out of your mind?

Thomas finally sits on the sofa.

THOMAS Maybe.

(beat)

I have weird souvenirs. Like I was dead and came back to life.

LINDA

Thomas. Promise me to never do it again.

THOMAS I promise.

LINDA

(sharply) Swear it.

THOMAS

(rolling his eyes and sighing) Cross my heart. (beat)

Tell me, do we know someone called something like McKenna?

Linda sits at her turn.

LINDA McKenna?

She shakes her head.

LINDA Nope. Why?

THOMAS

Since I woke up, I strangely have that name in mind and a city: BatonRouge.

LINDA

Stop the whisky, would you?

THOMAS

It's crazy, but that dream was really strong, almost real.

LINDA

(innocently) Was it in color?

But Thomas dose not listen to her.

THOMAS

I had a feeling of happiness, quietness--

LINDA

(trying to joke) What kind of pills did you take?

THOMAS I was in Heaven.

LINDA Why did you come back then?

Thomas is about to answer when someone knocks on his door. A bit surprised, he steps to the door and gives an eye in the peephole to see-ANGELA'S DISTORTED FACE She stands in front his door, straight-faced.

Pale, Thomas cannot believe it. He gives a second look and starts to panic. Linda does not understand.

LINDA

What's wrong? Who is it?

Thomas faces Linda and takes her by the shoulders, serious.

THOMAS

Linda. Do you trust me?

LINDA

Yes, but--

THOMAS

(interrupting)

The Two Angels

No question please.

ANOTHER KNOCK ON THE DOOR

Thomas disappears into a room and comes back with a bag.

THOMAS Follow me.

He takes his jacket and a scarf, opens the living room window, and passes a leg outside. From behind the door, Angela's voice rises.

ANGELA (V.O.)

Thomas! I know you're here!

Linda looks at Thomas as if he was some kind of lunatic, halfamused. He is already outside. She decides to follow him.

EXT. STREET - THOMAS' BUILDING - DAY

Thomas steps into the snow, followed by Linda.

LINDA

I never saw you running from a girl. Who's she?

THOMAS

I said no question, okay?

LINDA

(shrugging) Okay.

(beat)

Are you going to leave your window open?

THOMAS

(not listening) Where's your car?

She shows him a red New Beetle and opens it automatically with her keys. Thomas rushes in it and slams the passenger door.

EXT. STREET - INT. LINDA'S CAR - DAY

Linda enters the car at her turn, starts the engine, and turns to Thomas.

LINDA Now?

Thomas thinks for a short while.

THOMAS

Take me to the airport.

LINDA Sure?

Thomas just nods. As Linda speeds up, Thomas turns back to his building entrance.

NO TRACE OF ANGELA

FADE TO BLACK:

EXT. STREETS - INT. CAB - DAY

Scott and Charli are seated at the back of a cab, both silent.

Charli looks by the window and apparently avoids Scott's eyes. She's very pale and tired. Scott looks rather nervous.

SCOTT

Did you think about it?

Charli emerges from her thoughts and turns to him with a sad smile.

CHARLI Sorry?

SCOTT

(smiling)

Did you think about our baby's name?

A long beat.

CHARLI

Listen Scott, I don't know.

SCOTT

Don't know about the name or-- having a baby?

A long beat.

CHARLI

(tired)

Both, I guess.

Scott's smile fades as Charli turns back her face to the window.

SCOTT

Tell me. Do you blame me about the accident?

CHARLI

(without looking at him) Yes.

FADE TO BLACK:

EXT. VANCOUVER AIRPORT - INT. LINDA'S CAR - DAY

Linda and Thomas arrive in sight of Vancouver Airport.

The Two Angels

INT. VANCOUVER AIRPORT - DAY

Vancouver International Airport departures hall looks like Heaven's Gates. The same cosmopolitan crowd, the same announcements, the same escalators. The serenity in less.

Among the buzzing crowd, Thomas looks lost. Linda, on his tail, is still amused.

LINDA And now, Sir?

Thomas does not answer. He steps to an AIRLINE CLERK behind her counter. On his way, his foot kicks a bag and he nearly stumbles.

THOMAS (to the airline clerk)

Next flight to Baton-Rouge?

The woman checks on her computer screen, then smiles to Thomas.

AIRLINE CLERK Gate fourteen. 14:11. Flight

Continental Airlines. Last call.

Linda joins Thomas.

LINDA

What are you doing down in Louisiana?

THOMAS

I don't know but I'm sure I must get there.

AIRLINE CLERK How will you be paying?

He searches in his pockets.

THOMAS

(to Linda)

Forgot my wallet. Lend me some cash.

LINDA

No way. I'm coming with you!

THOMAS

But--

LINDA

(interrupting)

You want my dinero? I'm coming with you!

Stuck, Thomas gives in. Suddenly aware that Angela could appear at any minute, he urges Linda. She turns to the airline clerk with her most charming smile.

Anxious, Thomas turns back and scans the hall. Angela could be anywhere. Every woman could turn to be her.

Linda keeps on talking with the woman. She looks like flirting. Thomas turns back to her and pulls her by the sleeve. She has the two air tickets in hand.

LINDA

(victorious)

I have her phone number.

But Thomas does not listen to her, already heading for Gate 14.

INT. CONTINENTAL AIRLINES PLANE - DAY

The Two Angels

Thomas and Linda are seated side by side inside a crowded 747. Thomas nervously sketches on one of the company magazine margin page--

Charli'S FACE

Then, he looks through the porthole, lost in his thoughts. Linda turns to him with a smile and notices the drawing.

Then, she turns to the plane central alley, intensely watching--

ONE OF THE STEWARDESSES' BUTT

FADE TO:

INT. CHARLI'S HOUSE - BEDROOM - DAY

Charli is seated, alone, on her bed. Someone knocks on the door. She sadly stares a the MP3 player.

JODEE (V.O.)

Charli, it's me, JoDee.

CHARLI Come in.

JODEE enters the bedroom. The freckles on her face prove she is a real pretty young red-haired woman. She closes back the door and steps to Charli.

JODEE How are you?

Charli grins a smile that means "so-so".

JODEE

Do you want me to leave you alone?

No, JoDee. I need someone to talk with. I've been silent for so many years, wrapped into some kind of invisible second skin. Today, I really don't know where I'm going to.

JoDee sits on the bed by Charli.

JODEE

I just met Scott before he leaves to work. He looks devastated. So guilty. I never saw him like that. (beat)

Do you think you will ever forgive him?

CHARLI

(sighing)

I don't think so. Something's broken in me. It was as if that accident had woke me up from some kind of deep lethargy.

(bitterly chuckling) As if I was living like a zombie until then. I can see clearly now.

JODEE

Don't tell me you're going to leave him after ten years of marriage?

CHARLI

I don't know. We shared so many things. I'll feel lost without him. But, he's not the Prince Charming I used to know anymore. I want to be somebody's hero. Feeling myself, talking aloud.

As she talks, Charli seems to recover.

JODEE

(happily)

Okay. Let's list his pros and cons like we used to do when we were teens.

Charli grins a smile.

JODEE

First, the pros.

Charli thinks with exaggeration and sighs.

CHARLI He makes me laugh.

JoDee counts "one" with her thumb.

JODEE

Good point. Then?

Charli tries to think about something, but cannot find another reason and shakes her head.

JODEE

At least, is he-- G.I.B.?

Charli does not get it.

JODEE

Well, you know-- G.I.B.

She taps on the mattress. Charli still does not understand.

JODEE

(finally)

Is he good in bed?

CHARLI Ah, this? Well, yes. (beat)

I can't tell you. I only knew him.

The Two Angels

He was my first one.

JODEE

You mean you never-- with another man?

CHARLI

(shaking her head)

No. I never needed shopping around. That's why I married him.

JoDee sighs.

JODEE

Okay. If you can't compare, let's proceed differently. Do you usually reach orgasm with him?

CHARLI

(embarrassed)

I think so. I've never asked myself that kind of question.

JODEE

(dumbfounded)

You're not even sure? That's quite important. Every couple's sex life should be fulfilled. Like one plus one equal one.

Talk about yourself. You're single for months.

JODEE

That's just because I haven't find my Mister Right yet. But we talk about you, Charli. What about your G-Spot?

CHARLI My--?

JODEE

(sighing)

It's the most important thing man's discovered for women. Imagine a switch you press on that lights on up inside you and--

(in front of Charli's puzzled stare)

Forget it. I'll lend you my books.

(beat) That's all for the pros?

CHARLI Think so.

JODEE Now, the cons.

This time, Charli does not take her time to answer.

CHARLI

He told he wasn't ready to have a baby. We don't listen to the same music, don't watch the same movies. We usually don't go out together. He has his own friends. He never wanted me to work. Not even a McJob. I just stay at home, waiting for him, watching soaps, or doing-- nothing.

JODEE

(grave)

I know. Always hurt me to see you like this.

CHARLI

(chuckling)

All it matters to him are the three "B".

JODEE The what?

(talking to herself)

The three "B". That motto rules his life: "beer, bowling, and blowjobs".

(sigh) Yeah, that's perfectly resumes him.

Can you picture this?

JODEE I never could figure all this out.

You seemed so happy together, the perfect pair. Everyone envied you.

CHARLI

I was just playing his game. What else could I do?

JODEE You could run away.

CHARLI Never had the guts.

JoDee stares at her for a while, silent.

JODEE

And if someone would ask you to? If someone would get you out from this squalor?

CHARLI

I'm some kind of prisoner. Who could find me here, in the boondocks?

Suddenly, JoDee gets excited.

JODEE

Listen Charli. I've got an idea. You remember my big sister Lou? She moved in Texas. She always begged me to join her. Let's go together, get a real life and our own three "B": boys, boys and boys!

CHARLI

(hesitating)

What about Scott? I just can't leave him without an explanation?

JODEE

Will he let you go? You'll think about it later. If you'll miss him, it will be always time to come back. And believe me, he will forgive you and grovel before you.

I don't know.

JODEE

Move your butt, baby. You'll find someone. You're still young. You're cute and smart. And you know the saying: too many men, so less time.

(beat)

I've heard that a woman placed an ad in the paper, saying, "husband wanted". The next day she received two hundred e-mails, saying "Take mine".

Charli cannot help laughing.

JODEE

I love to see you laugh. That's the little Charli I used to know.

CHARLI I need it so bad. (thinking)

I have to tell you something I will never tell Scott. Maybe you'll find me crackbrained, but from my coma, I still have unclear memories. A face lost in a crowd. A man's face. For a while, I'm sure I felt myself happy, then desperate. So strange. I even remember telling him "thank you" but I don't know why.

JODEE

(excited)

You mean you met someone up there? Weird place for a date.

CHARLI

I told you, you would find me crazy.

JODEE

No, no. I do believe in these things. I've read a lot about it. Maybe you came back to Earth to find him?

CHARLI

Yes, but If I met him up there, that's mean he's dead now.

JoDee's exaltation falls back.

JODEE

You're probably right. Well, that's another reason you have nothing to lose to run away with me. You need wide open spaces, to see new faces. A brand new life is offered to you.

This time full of happiness and laughs.

Charli is about to speak. JoDee interrupts her.

JODEE

(smiling)

Yes. I know. You don't know.

FADE TO BLACK:

INT. BATON-ROUGE METROPOLITAN AIRPORT - DAY

Thomas and Linda are in Baton-Rouge Airport arrivals hall.

They obviously too much dressed up for the local weather. Thomas looks for the exit.

EXT. BATON-ROUGE METROPOLITAN AIRPORT - DAY

Thomas and Linda catch a taxi. The car speeds up.

INT. RICHMOND SUITES HOTEL - ROOM - DAY
Thomas and Linda enter a hotel room. Linda is sweating.

LINDA

You do what you want but I'm taking a shower. I'm creased!

As she disappears into the bathroom, Thomas notices a computer by the TV set. He switches it on, types on the keyboard and finds the White Pages site. He keeps typing and a list of names appears on the screen.

CLOSE-UP ON THE SCREEN

There are eight McKennas in Baton-Rouge.

Thomas sighs. He prints the page.

LINDA (V.O.)

The Two Angels

(from the bathroom)

Thomas! Don't you think I've been patient enough? Can't you tell me now what it's all about?! I really feel like a puppet with you!

Thomas is rummaging through Linda's purse and takes some cash. With the printed page, he steps out, slamming the door.

EXT. RICHMOND SUITE HOTEL - DAY

In front of the hotel, Thomas hails a cab where he steps in.

EXT. HOUSE - BATON-ROUGE STREET - DAY

SILENT SEQUENCE

Thomas is talking with a WOMAN on her threshold. The woman shakes her head. Disappointed, Thomas leaves her.

INT. BUILDING LOBBY - DAY

SILENT SEQUENCE

An OLD MAN slams his door on Thomas' surprised face.

EXT. TRAILER - BATON-ROUGE STREET - DUSK

SILENT SEQUENCE

Thomas is talking with a much EFFEMINATE GUY who does not stop to smile at him, visibly flirting. He looks like inviting Thomas in who refuses, rushing back to the street.

INT. RICHMOND SUITES HOTEL - LOBBY - NIGHT

As soon as Thomas enters the hotel lobby, a voice calls him.

The Two Angels

LINDA (O.S.) Thomas!

She stands inside the hotel bar. She is seated in a booth, drinking a cocktail.

INT. RICHMOND SUITES HOTEL - BAR - NIGHT

Thomas steps to her and joins her in the booth.

LINDA

Where the hell have you been? I was worrying to death.

THOMAS Looking for someone.

LINDA

(serious)

Don't you think you owe me some serious explanations?

THOMAS

I'm not sure you'd quite understand.

LINDA

Hey! Call me stupid. I'm not a blonde! And most of all, I'm your best friend.

THOMAS

Okay. But, promise me you will not laugh at me.

(beat)

Just after you left on Christmas Eve-FADE TO:

LATER

THOMAS

--and I finally checked three of them this afternoon.

Thomas and Linda are now both drinking.

LINDA This is insane.

THOMAS

Always told you I was.

LINDA

No, I mean, you should really believe in your story to be here, in a town you don't know.

THOMAS Do you?

LINDA

Can't tell you. If it wasn't you, I sure would think you're loco.

Suddenly, Thomas freezes and spills his glass on his trousers. Linda follows his eyes. A woman has just entered the bar-ANGELA

She still wears her long black coat. She slowly walks directly to Thomas. He does not know what to do, jammed.

ANGELA

(austere)

Thomas. We have to talk.

Linda rearranges her hair, takes a charming pose, and keeps staring at Angela.

LINDA

(to Thomas) Don't you introduce me?

Thomas feels increasingly trapped.

THOMAS

Linda, this is-- Angela.

Linda holds her hand out to Angela who does not move, just as if she wasn't there.

LINDA

(with a come-hither look) Pleased to meet you. Thomas' friends are mine too.

She sizes Angela up, trying to guess her shapes under her coat.

ANGELA

Thomas, that's really important.

Thomas starts to dry his trousers up with a napkin.

THOMAS

(confused) Yes.

ANGELA

Can we talk-- in private?

Linda gets up.

LINDA Okay. Got it.

As she steps to the counter, Angela sits down, facing Thomas.

ANGELA

(gently)

The Two Angels

You know why I'm here, don't you? No need to refresh your mind?

THOMAS

(firmly)

I don't want to go back.

You have to. You don't belong here anymore. Don't you realize what have you done?

Thomas nods.

THOMAS

I do. Look at me, I'm fine. I've got plenty of friends and--

ANGELA

(interrupting)

Don't do this to me, Thomas. I know now everything about you and why you have committed suicide.

THOMAS Who are you?

ANGELA

You perfectly know who I am. Let's call me an angel.

THOMAS

Alright, you're an angel. Fine to me. If you know everything about me, then, explain to me why I'm here?

ANGELA

Because you don't know what you're missing above, freed from your skin. Because you're still holding to this miserable life of yours like every human being. There are millions of reasons--

THOMAS (with a smile)

Sorry, you're wrong.

Angela is quite surprised. She beckons Thomas to give her his hand.

ANGELA May I?

Thomas gives her his hand. Angela holds it and closes her eyes for a short while. Thomas turns to Linda who stares at them, astonished.

FLASHBACK - INT. HEAVEN'S GATE - NIGHT

THOMAS' P.O.V.: as he speaks with Angela, Thomas turns a last time to Charli.

She grins a little helpless smile and mouths "Thank you" to him. Thomas can see regrets in her eyes as she slightly waves to him before she disappears into the shining fog.

END OF THE FLASHBACK:

INT. RICHMOND SUITES HOTEL - BAR - NIGHT

Thomas turns back to Angela who reopens her eyes.

ANGELA

That's because of her? The woman on the escalator?

THOMAS

You see. You can't know everything. (trying to joke)

I'm full of surprises.

Angela looks embarrassed.

ANGELA

Well, I have to be straight with you Thomas. If I don't get you back, my hierarchy would be quite angry with me. And that would be the first time for me in eight hundred years.

She lowers her head.

ANGELA

In fact, I maybe won't be able to go back at all.

Thomas looks at her, dumbfounded.

ANGELA

You broke Heaven's law Thomas. No one has ever escaped.

THOMAS

(happily surprised) You mean I'm the first one? I'm rather proud of it.

ANGELA

(straight-faced)

That's not the question. This is a very serious situation.

THOMAS

Listen--

Confused, he tries to remember her name.

Angela.

THOMAS

Angela, if I came back it's only to find that woman. I don't know if as an-- angel, you can feel love, but that's what I felt when I saw her. I've got to find her. I'm ready to give up everything I own.

Angela is about to speak.

THOMAS

Everything, except my life. (beat)

I admit I made a mistake. I shouldn't have commit suicide. I was wrong. But, let's suppose for a second that God Himself gave me this opportunity to make up for it. To give me a second chance. Meeting her above. Escaping from there. It just can't be coincidences.

Angela stares at him, thoughtful.

ANGELA Just one second.

She gets up and, as she steps to the back of the room, she takes out from her coat pocket some kind of cellular phone. She unfolds it and puts it at her ear.

Thomas stares at her and turns to Linda who beckons him "What's going on?".

He shrugs and faces back Angela who turns her back to him, speaking with a low voice on the phone. She hangs up and sighs.

She stays immobile for a short while and steps back to Thomas to sit down.

ANGELA

I have permission to make a special agreement with you. You have seven days to find her and be loved in return or you will go back up without a chance to be ever reincarnated or being an angel.

THOMAS

(happy) Okay.

Does the word purgatory mean something to you?

THOMAS

I missed most of my Sunday school.

ANGELA

(serious)

I guessed. Sojourn in Purgatory is greater than the pain that you've ever experienced in life. Every day you suffered would be multiply by ten.

THOMAS And you told me there was not Hell?

Big deal.

(grave)

But, she worth it. I won't fail this time.

(self confident)

I go for it. Do I have to sign with my blood?

ANGELA

(chuckling)

Who do you think you are? Some kind of Faust? No. Your word has just been taken for granted.

(beat)

I have to precise you also that you'll find her but I won't help you in this quest.

THOMAS

Why? Are you going to tail me all the way?

ANGELA

Yes. I have to. I don't want to have to chase you everywhere around the planet.

THOMAS

(charming)

Fine to me. I couldn't have a nicest angel to chaperon me.

Angela is blushing. Thomas notices it.

ANGELA (another topic)

By the way, you forgot this in your apartment.

She hands him a wallet.

I know that you Earthling, you desperately need it.

THOMAS Thank you.

He slips it into his pocket.

ANGELA A last thing.

She turns to Linda.

ANGELA

Could you-- gently-- get rid of her?

THOMAS

But, she helped me till now and--

ANGELA

(interrupting)

Make something up. You're a story maker, aren't you? Tell her I'm one of your ex-girlfriend.

THOMAS

(sarcastic)

You just ask me to lie? Isn't it a sin?

ANGELA

(embarrassed)

Well, not a deadly one.

He stands up and walks to Linda.

ANGELA'S P.O.V.

Linda looks disappointed and, reluctantly, she nods. She hugs Thomas, turns to Angela, and whispers something to him that makes him laugh. Then, she leaves the bar.

Thomas comes back to Angela, still laughing.

ANGELA

What did she tell you so funny?

THOMAS

I really can't tell you. You wouldn't appreciate that.

ANGELA Come on Thomas.

She was only talking about a special part of your body.

FADE TO BLACK:

INT. CHARLI'S HOUSE - NIGHT

A door opens and Scott appears, a bunch of roses in hand. The house is dark and quiet. Scott closes the door.

SCOTT Honeybunch!?

NO ANSWER

He switches on the lights, puts the flowers on a table, and starts to worry.

SCOTT Charli?!

THERE ARE NO CHRISTMAS DECORATIONS IN THE HOUSE

He opens the bedroom door. Charli is not there. He explores the entire house and enters the bathroom.

INT. CHARLI'S HOUSE - BATHROOM - NIGHT

Something looks like to bother him. In a flash, he notices that half of the shelves are empty. He rushes out.

SCOTT (O.S.) Charli!!

INT. CHARLI'S HOUSE - BEDROOM - NIGHT

(MORE)

Scott enters the bedroom and opens the wardrobe. All Charli's stuff has disappeared. Scott's fist hits the wardrobe door and goes through.

Pale, he steps backward to the bed and collapses on it. He feels something under him and takes the small MP3 player and an envelop out.

Trembling, he opens it and starts to read.

CHARLI (V.O.)

"Dear Scott. I'm gone maybe for a while, maybe for longer. I really don't know. I have to think about all this. I'm sure you'll take good care of you.

CHARLI(cont'd)

Maybe it's just a single battle lost, but not the war. I hope you'll understand that I have changed. Please, believe me when I tell that I will always love you. Charli."

A tear runs on Scott's cheek. He lets himself fall back on the bed, and closes his eyes.

FADE TO BLACK:

INT. RICHMOND SUITES HOTEL - DINNING ROOM - NIGHT

In the hotel dinning room, Thomas and Angela face each other at a dinner table. Thomas is the only one to eat. In fact, he rather looks to gobble down.

THOMAS

(full mouth)

I could eat an entire cow. God, I'm starving.

(to Angela)

Are you on the diet?

ANGELA

I don't need to eat anymore.

THOMAS

You mean you don't know how a cheeseburger or a crepe suzette taste? What a shame.

Angela shakes her head with a smile.

THOMAS

Don't drink neither?

He raises his glass of wine.

THOMAS Well. Cheers.

He drinks up.

THOMAS

Sure you don't want to have just a sip. It's refreshing and sweet. You don't know what you're missing.

ANGELA

I usually quench my thirst differently. Wisdom is my only nectar.

Thomas stares at her, grimacing.

Tell me. Does everybody talk through parables where you come from?

ANGELA

(with a smile) An old habit from the boss.

(more seriously)

So, Thomas, did you start your seeking already?

THOMAS

Yeah. They're eight to have the same name in Baton-Rouge. I've already met three of them. I'll meet the five left tomorrow.

ANGELA I wish you good luck then.

THOMAS

Thank you--

(worried)

Wait. You seem too much self confident.

ANGELA

(innocently) Do I?

THOMAS

You can't wish me good luck when you absolutely want to bring me back with you by any means. You're up onto something.

He frowns.

THOMAS

Do you just actuate people to lie or are you a liar yourself?

ANGELA

We, angels, are not allowed to lie.

CLOSE-UP ON ANGELA'S CROSSED FINGERS IN HER BACK

THOMAS

One thing I finally know about you. That's not fair. I have no secret for you and I just know your name.

Who were you when you lived?

ANGELA

(elusive) I forgot.

THOMAS Tss, tss. Remember, you can't lie.

ANGELA

Okay. I was a peasant girl in the

South of France. I died giving birth to a beautiful baby who never knew her mother.

Thomas has stopped eating and he listens to her with a real interest.

THOMAS

That's fascinating.

He puts his elbow on the table, holding his chin. But he misses the table edge and nearly falls. He stiffens on the back of his chair and stays still.

ANGELA

It is not. I was living in misery. People were dying very young at this time. Death and woe were everywhere.

THOMAS

So, since then you're an angel.

ANGELA

The Two Angels

(embarrassed)

Speak lower, please.

THOMAS

But, people don't care nowadays.

He suddenly gets up and shouts throughout the dinning room.

THOMAS

Hey! She's an angel!! My angel!!

CUSTOMERS turn their heads with a smile and are finally back to their dinner as if nothing had happened. Thomas sits back and starts to eat again.

THOMAS

You see?

(beat)

Let's suppose you walk up to a cop and say: "Hi, I'm Angela and I'm your guardian angel." Well, you'd find yourself spending your night in a drunk tank.

He drinks a sip of wine.

You see, people don't believe in anything anymore. I was the same. Sometimes, I was worrying about money, sometimes I wished to have no shoe, no shirt and no problem.

(beat)

The Two Angels

People have lost faith. Too many wars, too many diseases, too much misery around. By the way, aren't you supposed to guide us from above?

ANGELA

Man still has his free will. That's makes all the difference. We try to guide you, but, most of the time, you decide to just not listen to us. Sometimes, we had no alternative. We have to act. We give man visions he believes in to help him to take the right decision. It's so strong that you actually assume it's true. That's what you call awaken dream.

THOMAS Is there really free will then?

ANGELA

As you said, you don't believe anymore.

Thomas looks at his watch.

THOMAS

It's getting late. I must find her quick. The clock is ticking for me.

He gets up.

THOMAS

If you excuse me.

Angela gets up too.

THOMAS

Where are you going?

ANGELA

(naturally) With you?

THOMAS

(shrugging) Okay.

He paces out the dinner room. Angela simply follows him.

FADE TO:

EXT. HIGHWAY - INT. JODEE'S CAR. NIGHT

On a desert highway, through the night, JoDee drives a threedoor coupe. Smooth Country music gently plays on the radio.

By her side, on the passenger seat, Charli sleeps, her head reclined against the window. For a short while, JoDee turns to her with a smile and keeps driving, humming along with the music.

INT. RICHMOND SUITES HOTEL - ROOM - NIGHT

From behind a door, a shower noise can be heard with Thomas happily humming. Angela is simply seated on an armchair, still wearing her black coat.

The shower noise ceases and Thomas appears, his hair wet, wearing a bathrobe. He towels off his hair.

THOMAS

You sure you ain't too hot with your coat?

ANGELA I'm fine.

THOMAS

(joking)

Are you going to sing me a lullaby? (chuckling)

It's weird. Are you going to watch me sleeping all night long?

She's about to answer.

THOMAS

Let me guess. You neither don't need to sleep.

She just nods. Thomas sits on the bed, sizing her up.

THOMAS

What do you need then?

ANGELA

Nothing. We're not supposed to be material. We only take a body to welcome newcomers or, when it needs, to fulfill our mission down there. (amazed)

You mean there are other angels on Earth?

ANGELA Of course, there are.

THOMAS

Do you know one called Clarence Oddbody?

ANGELA Who?

THOMAS

(shaking his head) Forget it. It's just a joke.

Angela hardly moves, even blinks.

THOMAS

Are you always that stiff? I mean, why don't you try to relax and enjoy your stay with me. You're sure you don't want to take your coat off?

Reluctantly, Angela takes her coat off. She wears a neat cotton dress, revealing agreeable shapes. She is clearly aware of Thomas' trouble she causes and smiles. A long beat.

THOMAS

A question haunts me for years. I'm sure you can answer. Are ghosts real?

ANGELA

What you call ghosts are in fact wandering souls, men and women, who are not aware to be dead. Lot of them couldn't find the right path and keep acting as if they were still alive and suffering.

THOMAS

Do they surround us? Can't they see everything we do?

Angela scans the room.

ANGELA

Yes. But just a few of them can reach the material world. They're the ones you call ghosts or spirits.

THOMAS

Spooky. When I think now I won't go to the toilets without company.

Angela smiles and takes off her shoes.

ANGELA

I'm still not used of that carnal envelope.

She spreads her toes.

The Two Angels

ANGELA I feel better.

After a long beat, she takes a serious pose.

ANGELA

What do you like in her?

THOMAS

I really can't tell. It was like I finally reached a safe haven. As if I always knew her. I was feeling warm inside. Retrieving my child soul. I was a new me.

ANGELA

But, you don't know her. This is not love. Sounds rather sexual impulse to me.

THOMAS

What do you know about love?

ANGELA

Which love? The earthling love or the spiritual one?

THOMAS

They're both equal to me. You can feel them burning into your chest. They both make you fall on your knees and be insignificant. The one you love can be a real deity for you.

ANGELA You're on the verge of the blasphemy.

(shaking his head)

I don't think so. In both cases, you can feel respect and humility for the one you love, God or a person.

ANGELA

The Two Angels

However, I know you knew greed and envy in your life. You've been jealous, cheating and--

THOMAS

(shrugging) Nobody's perfect. Were you?

Angela does not know what to reply.

THOMAS

I always wished to be as pure as I could reflect myself in-- an angel's tear. But, life down there is so. You rapidly give in and forget. Christian precepts are wonderful, but no more applicable in today life. No one can be a saint anymore. Well, maybe Mother

Teresa was. (beat)

You know, I thought about it before I decided to kill myself. My conclusion was I didn't belong to my time. I was too old-fashioned. Too softie like Linda would say. And awkward too. That's why every girl managed to break my heart. (beat)

But when I saw her eyes, the way she looked at me, and that despair on her face, everything became clear to me. She was meant for me. I had no second thought. I had to

find her and make her happy. And here I am.

Angela stays thoughtful for a while.

ANGELA

(shaking her head) You can't be right.

THOMAS

Think what you want. I have to sleep now, if you please.

The Two Angels

He switches out the light, takes his bathrobe off, and lies into the sheets.

THOMAS (V.O.) Good night Angela.

ANGELA (V.O.) Good night Thomas.

ANGELA'S P.O.V.

As if she was wearing infrared glasses, Angela can see through the darkness. She scans Thomas' body. As he rolls back and turns to her, she stares at his face.

CHARLI'S DREAM

A succession of quick shots in Charli's P.O.V.:

-        Scott drinking behind his wheel

-        the car crash

-        Charli stuck inside the car's wreck

-        a bright white light that blinds her

-        as the bright white light fades the frame turns to negative

-        a crowd with many faces and an unclear voice from loudspeakers

-        the steps of an escalator

-        Thomas' face- then the bright light again and a voice in echo:

JODEE (V.O.) Charli. Charli!

EXT. GAS STATION - INT. JODEE'S CAR - DAY

As Charli wakes up, a bright sunray blinds her.

JODEE

Charli, wake up!

JoDee is outside the car in a gas station.

JODEE

God. You were sleeping so deeply.

Charli stretches up.

CHARLI Where are we?

JODEE

Wichita Falls. Four more hours to go. I'm exhausted. Mind to drive?

CHARLI

I'll be alright after a nice cup of coffee.

She steps out of the car and yawns.

CHARLI

I had one of my best nights for years. No bad dream. No stress.

Just letting myself go.

JODEE

I saw that. (beat)

Didn't you know you are talking in your sleep?

Charli shakes her head.

JODEE

You kept saying "Thank you".

CHARLI I can't remember.

She shivers.

CHARLI Spooky.

They step to the gas station store.

FADE TO:

INT. CHARLI'S HOUSE - LIVING ROOM - DAY

Scott is reclined over the living room table, sleeping and snoring, an empty bottle of scotch by him.

The doorbell rings. Scott does not move.

RING

Scott grunts and raises his head. He is badly shaved.

RING

SCOTT

(shouting) Alright! 'coming!

He gets up and walks to the small lobby where he opens the front door. He faces Thomas and, a few steps behind, Angela. Blinded by the daylight, he raises his hand on the forehead.

SCOTT Yeah?

THOMAS

I'm looking for Mrs. McKenna.

SCOTT

(aggressive)

Not at home. I'm her hubby. What do ya want?

He looks at Angela in her long black coat.

SCOTT Ya're FBI?

Thomas frowns and shakes his head.

THOMAS

No, no. We're just-- friends of her.

SCOTT

(woozy)

I don't know ya. If you're friends of her, find her then. She left me. Gone. Kaput!

THOMAS Where is she?

SCOTT

(bitterly)

Back to Hell where she should have better stay.

THOMAS

What do you mean?

SCOTT

She came back from the dead with some eerie ideas and flew away. She said she'd always love me. She'll be back.

THOMAS

You don't have the slightest idea where she could be?

Angela notices that Scott is clenching his fists. She gently pulls Thomas' arm.

SCOTT It's none of your damn business!

Buzz off and leave me alone!

He slams the door on Thomas' nose. He's nearly crying, foaming inside.

SCOTT

(to himself) Leave me alone.

EXT. BATON-ROUGE STREETS - INT. TAXICAB - DAY

Thomas and Angela are seated on a taxicab back seat. As the CAB DRIVER speeds through the street, Thomas looks bewildered.

THOMAS

(almost to himself) That is the story of my life. As soon as I get something I'm holding on, I lose it.

He looks desperate and turns to Angela.

THOMAS

Okay. Dice have rolled. I'm ready to follow you.

Angela looks at him with some kind of pity.

ANGELA

I don't get you. You let it down at the first occasion.

THOMAS

The Two Angels

What can I do? She's gone. I have no clue of where she could be. Look at me. I was stupid to think that it would be a walkover. That she would wait for me. It never crossed my mind she could be married or even less, she could be nowhere to be found.

He reclines his head against the cab window, blue in the face, his eyes lost. They stay silent for a while.

Angela cannot help looking at him, sorry. She sighs.

ANGELA

Let's suppose you're a woman and you're leaving home. Where generally would you flee to when things go wrong?

THOMAS

I don't know. When there's no place to go-- To her folks?

She simply agrees. A phone rings resounds inside the cab. Obviously, Angela's phone. She does not answer, in front of Thomas' amazed look.

ANGELA

(shrugging)

They'll leave a message.

THOMAS

I thought you weren't supposed to help me?

The telephone stops ringing.

ANGELA

You guessed it by yourself. Aren't you?

(looking towards the sky) He guessed it by himself.

THOMAS

Big deal. Where shall I find her parents?

Angela closes her eyes for a while.

CAB DRIVER

1137 Covenant Drive? Yes, Ma'am.

As Thomas turns to her, she innocently puts her hand on her mouth.

ANGELA Oops...

FADE TO BLACK:

Her telephone RINGS again.

EXT. HIGHWAY - INT. JODEE'S CAR - DAY

As Charli now drives, she and JoDee happily sing along the Country rock song on the radio. They shake their heads and wildly toss their hair.

CHARLI & JODEE

(singing at unison)

Girls with guitars, there ought to be a song about, girls with guitars, there's just no stopping those girls with guitars get your

money for nothing and your guys for

    free--

Charli's troubles seem forgotten.

On the highway, a road sign reads AMARILLO.

EXT. CHARLI'S PARENTS HOUSE - DAY

An old house decorated with multicolored shells. The taxicab pulls over the gate. Thomas and Angela step out of the taxi. Thomas pays and walks to Angela as the taxi speeds away.

THOMAS

Why did you help me?

ANGELA

I can't stand seeing a human being suffering. I never could.

THOMAS

(keenly)

You'll have a lot of job to do down there.

They enter the garden and pace to the front door where Thomas presses the ring at the door. A lady in her mid-fifties opens. She's VIOLET, Charli's mother. She looks tired.

VIOLET Yes? Can I help you?

THOMAS

Hi. My name is Thomas Hanson and I'm looking for your daughter.

VIOLET Charli?

Thomas turns to Angela who simply nods.

THOMAS Yes, Charli.

Violet stares at them for a short while.

VIOLET

The Two Angels

Are you with the FBI?

Thomas cannot help smiling.

THOMAS

No, no. Just friends of her. May we-- come in?

Violet stares at Thomas.

VIOLET

You have a good face. Come in.

Thomas and Angela enter the house.

INT. CHARLI'S PARENTS HOUSE - LIVING ROOM - DAY

The rooms are dull and poorly decorated. It looks as if time has stopped inside these walls. Violet leads Thomas and Angela to the living-room where the TV is on by a tinyChristmas tree.

In front of the TV, in a wheelchair watching Joyce Meyer on God TV, a man in his early sixties is seated. GEORGE, cannot talk anymore.

VIOLET

Please, sit down.

They three sit down around the table.

THOMAS

Is-- Charli here?

VIOLET

The Two Angels

I wish. We haven't seen her for ten years. I hoped you would give me some news about her. When she met her husband, she decided she didn't need us anymore, that she had found her own family. We weren't even invited to the wedding.

She gets up and fixes them a cup of coffee.

VIOLET

Two years after, my husband George had a stroke. I tried to contact her but she even refused to talk to me.

(turning to the Christmas tree)

Since then, every Christmas, we keep a present for her just in case she would pop by.

Close up of a big present at the foot of the Christmas tree.

THOMAS

Maybe she will. I've heard she left her husband.

Violet sadly smiles and sits back.

VIOLET

I always knew she couldn't be happy with him. She was too stubborn to admit it.

ANGELA

There always are miracles on Christmas time.

VIOLET

Ten years I pray for one. I don't believe in miracles anymore.

ANGELA

The Two Angels

Don't give up your prayers. There is always someone to respond.

Telephone rings. Violet stands up and picks up the phone.

VIOLET

(on the phone)

Yes.

(beat)

Charli!? My princess! Are you okay?!

Thomas turns to Angela and beckons "Is that you?". She shakes her head.

VIOLET

(on the phone)

Of course, I'm glad hearing from you. Where are you? (beat)

Amarillo in Texas? What are you--?

EXT. AMARILLO STREET - INT. PHONE BOOTH - DAY

Charli stands in a phone booth. JoDee waits for her outside.

CHARLI

(on the phone)

Mom, I'm sorry. I've no much time. Just to say I love you, you and dad, and I'm okay. Don't worry anymore.

She hangs up and looks exhausted.

EXT. AMARILLO STREET - DAY

Charli steps out of the phone booth and comes to JoDee.

JODEE

So? Was it a good advice?

Charli smiles at her.

CHARLI Thank you.

JODEE

(proud of her) I was inspired.

She hands her the car keys.

INT. CHARLI'S PARENTS HOUSE - LIVING ROOM - DAY

Violet is seated back, febrile. She is almost shaking.

VIOLET

I never thought she would ever call.

She turns to her husband.

VIOLET If only he could know. (to Thomas)

She's with her girlfriend JoDee in Amarillo, in Texas. It looks like she finally had her move.

Thomas gets up.

THOMAS

I guess we're gonna leave you now to your hopes.

Violet takes his hand.

VIOLET

The Two Angels

My prayer now is that you'll bring her back to us. She would deserve you.

THOMAS

What do you mean?

VIOLET

I can see the love you feel for her in your eyes.

Puzzled, Thomas turns to Angela.

THOMAS

I only wish everyone would agree.

Angela gets up and steps to George. She simply puts her hand on his. The man smiles.

GEORGE

(hardly)

Thank-- you--

Violet cannot believe it. She rushes to George and knees by him.

VIOLET

(emotional)

Did you just talk?! Did you just talk?!

George raises his hand and puts it on her head, smiling. Violet turns to Thomas and Angela.

VIOLET What have you--

She stops. They are already gone.

FADE TO BLACK:

EXT. LOU'S RESIDENCE - INT. JODEE'S CAR - DAY

JoDee's coupé parks in front of a luxurious house made out of glass where the sun reflects.

CHARLI

You're sure you've got the right address?

JODEE Positive.

JoDee leans over to honk and a woman steps out of the house, laughing. She happily walks to the car. She's LOU (35), JoDee's sister, a tall blonde woman, the perfect "cow girl". She opens JoDee's door and happily hugs her.

LOU

Little sister! At last!

JoDee gets of the car, followed by Charli.

JODEE

Lou, this is Charli. Do you remember her?

Lou joins Charli and hugs at her turn.

LOU

Last time I saw you, you were wearing pig-tails and splashed around in your tiny plastic pool. Welcome to the Lone Star state girls!

They enter the house.

INT. LOU'S RESIDENCE - LIVING ROOM - DAY

The well-to-do and cozy interior of the house is entirely dedicated to the Country music. Several guitars are hanged on the walls. Charli cannot believe what she sees.

LOU

You can stay all the time you wish. Tim is so often out that it seems I live by myself.

JODEE

(to Charli)

Her husband is the Country singer Tim Spears. But Lou does not like we talk about it. That's why I never told you.

(with a smile) Sorry.

CHARLI

(impressed) Tim Spears?!

INT. LOU'S RESIDENCE - BEDROOM - DAY

They enter a sumptuous bedroom with silky wall covering.

LOU

(to Charli)

I guess this is your bedroom. No one else on Earth has ever slept here. You'll the first one.

Charli scans around the room with a king-size bed and silk sheets. On the walls, under frame, a dozen of gold records. She sits on the bed.

LOU

Waterbed. You don't mind?

The Two Angels

CHARLI

(impressed) No. Fine.

LOU Or I give you another bedroom.

CHARLI No. That's okay.

LOU

(to JoDee) I'll show yours, little sister.

Lou and JoDee step out of the bedroom, leaving Charli alone. She lies down, feeling good, and trying the waterbed.

INT. GREYHOUND TERMINAL - DUSK

In the Baton-Rouge Greyhound terminal hall, Thomas talkswith a CLERK behind his counter, his Visa in hand.

THOMAS

Two tickets for Amarillo.

CLERK

The bus leaves in two hours.

THOMAS Fine.

INT. BAR - NIGHT

Lou, JoDee and Charli are seated around a table in a bar where Country music plays loud. They drink Margaritas. Lou looks rather drunk.

LOU

Tim's gone for a three-month tour, including Canada. Though he calls me everyday, I feel alone. It's hard to be a Country singer's wife.

I'm glad you came to cheer me up. So, how things going in BatonRouge?

JODEE

(sighing)

As boring as usual.

LOU

And mom and dad?

JODEE

(concluding)

As boring as usual.

Lou laughs. JoDee notices TWO GUYS who drink at the counter. She pushes Charli's elbow.

JODEE What do you think?

Charli turns to them and just shrugs.

JODEE

(to Lou)

She broke with her husband yesterday after ten years of marriage. She needs some fun.

LOU

(to Charli)

The Two Angels

Cheer up Charli. You're not the first and not the last. Listen. Let's consider men like Kleenexes. You use them and throw them away first before they do. You see, Tim's my third husband and I'm not really sure if he's the good one. But, never mind. I enjoy! C'est la vie!

JODEE

(to Charli)

Yes! Enjoy! Remember the three "B"! Boys, boys and boys!

LOU

(to Charli)

Yeah, she's right! Have a drink! Don't give a damn!

CHARLI I don't give a damn!!

(raising her glass) To the Kleenexes!!

They three raise and clink their glasses.

FADE TO BLACK:

EXT. HIGHWAY - INT. BUS - NIGHT

As the bus speeds in the night, Thomas and Angela are seated side by side. Like an obsession, Thomas keeps sketching Charli's face on a scrapbook.

ANGELA

Why do people keep asking us if we're with the FBI?

THOMAS

It's the way you're dressed. They watched too much TV.

Angela nods to the scrapbook.

ANGELA

(looking at the scrapbook) You're really talented.

THOMAS

Wish everybody would think like you. It would be easier to sell my own comics.

ANGELA

Just believe in yourself, Thomas. That's how things work. It'll seem easier.

(beat)

Do you want me to talk about where I come from?

THOMAS

(shaking his head)

Nothing you could say would change my mind. I found my own Heaven down here with her.

INT. BAR - NIGHT

Lou, JoDee and Charli are dancing on the dance floor. They three look rather drunk and have fun. The two guys from the counter have joined them.

EXT. HIGHWAY - INT. BUS - NIGHT

Almost everyone sleeps in the bus that speeds into the night. Angela is still awake. She stares at Thomas who sleeps too, but her expression has changed.

Then, she shivers and takes her phone out from a coat.

(MORE)

ANGELA

(on the phone)

What now?

(beat)

What about my behavior? You told me I had carte blanche to bring him back. I have a plan and I WILL bring him back. Do not worry. (beat)

No, I don't feel anything for him. Just tenderness. Just like an angel to an Earthling soul. (beat)

Yes, I know I can't. That I would be severely reprimanded, but I'm just doing my task.

ANGELA(cont'd)

(beat)

Er... I've got static. I can't hear you and--

Irritated, she suddenly folds her phone up and sighs. Then, she turns again to Thomas with a tender smile. Her telephone hums again, but she does not answer. The phone ceases humming.

A telephone rings in her back. A GUY whispers on the seat just behind Angela and Thomas. The guy leans over to Angela, his cell phone in hand.

GUY

(whispering) Are you Angela?

Angela turns to him, ireful, and shakes her head. The guy sits back. The GIRL at his side wakes up.

GIRL (O.S.)

Who's on the phone? And who the Hell is this Angela?

By Thomas, Angela untied her bun and tosses her hair. The black locks wildly fall on her shoulders.

THOMAS' DREAM

In a big wheat field, a huge crowd made of HUNDRED OF WOMEN of all ages and races. Thomas is stuck in the middle, pushed by every woman he bumps into like a pinball ball.

As he is pushed ahead, the crowd gets disbanded to form a path like to a woman--

Charli

She stands in the middle of the wheat field and stares at Thomas with a smile. She slowly reaches out her hand to him.

Thomas starts to run to her, but, as the soil slunk under his feet, he falls into darkness in an endless dive. THOMAS SCREAMS

EXT. GREYHOUND TERMINAL - INT. BUS - DAWN
THOMAS' P.O.V.

Thomas opens his eyes. Angela's face enters the frame.

ANGELA Thomas! Are you alright?

Angela is leaned over him, her hair almost caressing his cheeks, smiling.

THOMAS

(almost panting) Where are we?

ANGELA

Amarillo. I tried to wake you up but you were far-gone.

He stares at her.

THOMAS

(confused) You look different. (beat) You hair--

ANGELA

(ingenuously)

I have just untied it.

Thomas' eyes have changed. The rising sun forms a halo-like around Angela's head. She seems to be aware of the effect she has on him.

ANGELA Something wrong?

THOMAS

(perturbed) No, no.

He gets up.

THOMAS

I'm gonna have a busy day.

Angela steps back from his way out and follows him.

INT. LOU'S RESIDENCE - BEDROOM - DAY

Charli is slowly waking up in her bed as someone gently knocks on the bedroom door. JoDee enters.

JODEE

(embarrassed)

Someone's there for you.

Surprised, Charli sits on the bed and stretches. She wears golden silk pajamas.

CHARLI Gimme two minutes.

She tries to recover from her sleep.

CHARLI Who is it?

JODEE

You'll see by yourself.

INT. LOU'S RESIDENCE - LIVING ROOM - DAY

Wrapped in a silky bathrobe over her pajamas, Charli enters the living room and sees--

SCOTT

He has a bunch of flowers in his hand. As soon as he sees Charli entering, he falls on one knee. He raises his flowers to her and starts to sing.

SCOTT

(singing)

I've just got to show you how differently I feel that I can be true to you that my love is real. But my past will forever haunt me if you say that you don't want me I'm down on my knees I'm begging you please, won't you? Have a change of heart Please have a, have a change of heart I see what I put you through I'll make it up to you--

His voice is trembling and he is obviously moved.

Charli is embarrassed. At first, she does not know what to do. Then she stares at him, totally inexpressive.

CHARLI

What are you doing here?

SCOTT

(smiling)

Take you back home, honeybunch. It is time. I've prepared you a welcome back party.

CHARLI

How did you find me?

SCOTT

JoDee's parents. I told them you forgot to give me your address to write.

(scanning around) Nice place.

CHARLI

(nervously chuckling) I hope you're joking?

SCOTT

(very calm)

No. I'm dead serious. You know, I rethought about all this over and over. You were right. I was stupid and childish. But I can change. You'll see. Trust me.

CHARLI

Do not start again. How many times we've been through this? You're gonna change. I'll see. Trusting you. No, Scott. Not this time. Game over. I can think by myself now.

SCOTT

But, you never gave me a single warning. How can you change like that? You even wanted a baby from me.

CHARLI

It wasn't "like that". Can't you figure one second what you did to me? I'm sure you can't. For once I can talk, I won't stay silent. You never let me talk, always answering for myself, thinking for myself.

Scott is about to speak.

CHARLI

Now, you're gonna listen to me. You wouldn't believe the days and nights I spent waiting for you, worrying. Expecting you weren't drunk again. (MORE)

Enduring your friends' stupid jokes. Feeling like a bauble. I've been silent too long. I want a real life. I want to gain back the youth you

stole away from me ten years ago! I wanna be born again!

Scott succeeds in remaining incredibly calm, though his eyes reflect rage and frustration.

SCOTT

Fine. Listen to me. I just got one thing to say. I'll be there if you need. Down deep inside of me I know you will be back. You still need me. You'd be nothing without me.

The Two Angels

SCOTT(cont'd)

I'll stay in town for a few days.

You know my number.

He takes the MP3 player out his pocket.

SCOTT

By the way, you forgot your present.

He quietly leaves the flowers and the MP3 player on the tiled floor and quietly steps out of the house.

JoDee looms from the corner where she was hidden.

JODEE

Wow! What a speech! I didn't recognize you. Congratulations girl!

They hug.

JODEE

You're shivering.

CHARLI I'm fine.

She heavily sighs.

CHARLI

I just hope I took the right decision.

They hug tighter.

JODEE

Don't worry. You did.

FADE TO:

The Two Angels

INT. HOLIDAY INN RECEPTION - DAY

Thomas and Angela enter a hotel reception hall. Angela has a very seductive way of walk and her blouse top is now unbuttoned. Everyone in the hall looks at her. She's radiant.

Thomas steps to the reception desk.

RECEPTIONIST Sir?

THOMAS

I'd like two rooms.

Angela joins him and takes his arm.

ANGELA

(to Thomas) Come on darling. Why two rooms?

(to the receptionist)

We're on honeymoon. He's a bit confused.

RECEPTIONIST Name?

THOMAS Hanson.

RECEPTIONIST

(typing on a computer) Mr. and Mrs. Hanson.

The receptionist holds a magnetic key to Thomas. Angela takes it from Thomas' hand.

ANGELA

I'm off to take a shower. Don't be too long. I miss you already.

She paces to the lift and turns back to send Thomas a kiss in front of his staggered look.

RECEPTIONIST

(to Thomas) Address?

INT. HOLIDAY INN - ROOM - DAY

Furious, Thomas enters the room. Angela is seated on the bed, relaxing.

THOMAS

What's that circus?! What game are you playing?!

ANGELA

(innocently)

Am I?

(seriously)

Maybe you're right. Life's not that bad down here. What harm does it make to have a little fun? If I have to stay a few days, I wanna make it my way too. I realized I'm missing my material life. Don't you understand this?

Thomas' anger ceases.

THOMAS Well.

(sigh)

Let's say it's quite comprehensible. Angela sighs.

ANGELA

(mothering)

Thomas, stop being that yes-man. You're too kind. That's your problem. Fight back sometimes. You can't go on in life being so laid down.

Thomas bends his head, shameful.

ANGELA

Promise me you will straight respond from now. You'll be more self-confident.

Thomas nods.

ANGELA

Hold your head up and respond!

THOMAS I will!

ANGELA

Good. Now, would you show me the bright side of life?

(with begging eyes) Please.

Thomas is about to speak.

ANGELA

(interrupting)

She'll wait for you just a few hours longer. Okay?

Thomas nods.

ANGELA (shaking her hair)

Good! I wanna born again!

FADE TO:

INT. DRESS STORE - DAY

MUSICAL SEQUENCE

The Two Angels

Thomas and Angela are in a store buying a dress for her. Several shots where Angela tries different dresses on and Thomas' appreciations.

As Angela appears in an beautiful dress, Thomas looks seduced. She is a really attractive woman.

LATER

It is now Thomas' turn to try some new costumes and be appreciated by Angela.

EXT. ROLLER COASTER - DAY

MUSICAL SEQUENCE

Thomas and Angela have fun riding a roller coaster.

EXT. AMARILLO STREET - DAY

MUSICAL SEQUENCE

Thomas and Angela listen to a Country music guitarist playing in the street.

INT. CAFE - DAY

MUSICAL SEQUENCE

Thomas and Angela are seated, in a cafe, both eating a giant ice-cream and laughing. Thomas wants Angela to taste his icecream. They exchange long intense looks. Thomas looks truly seduced.

MUSIC CEASES

Outside, Thomas has not seen Charli walking by with JoDee across the street.

EXT. AMARILLO STREET - DAY

Charli and JoDee rapidly walk down the street, chat, when they hear a voice calling.

SCOTT (O.S.)

(calling)

>   Honeybunch!

Charli turns her head and stops. Scott is crossing the street towards them, manifestly drunk.

SCOTT

(cynical)

My dear wife. The apples of my eyes. As you can see, your hubby is himself, boozy-woozy.

A car has to stop, its tires screeching.

SCOTT (to the car) Oh, easy does it pal!

He keeps coming to Charli and JoDee.

SCOTT

(to Charli)

Enough of your crap, now! You're my wife and this time you're coming back home with me!

JoDee interferes.

JODEE

Get away, you shuffler!

Scott threats to slap her but he holds his arm back.

SCOTT

(to JoDee)

Or what?! You're gonna spank me, bitch?! I'm sure she wouldn't have leave without you! It's all your fault!

(to Charli) Come with me!

CHARLI

(coldly)

It's over Scott. Even if I'd come back, I would run away again at the first occasion.

She takes her wedding ring from her finger and hands to Scott.

SCOTT

But you told me you'll always love me.

Scott pockets the ring.

CHARLI I will-- somehow.

She resumes walking with JoDee, leaving Scott.

SCOTT Honeybunch.

Charli and JoDee walk away.

SCOTT

(yelling)

Honeybunch! Honeybunch!!

INT. CAFE - DAY

Scott's voice is heard inside the cafe. Thomas turns his head to the street and sees Scott shouting. Looking whom he's yelling at, he notices the two young women walking away. HE RECOGNIZES Charli Without a word, he gets up and runs out.

EXT. CAFE - AMARILLO STREET - DAY

Thomas sprints out of the cafe and sees Charli turning around the corner. He crosses the street without attention, when he hears a car's tyres shrieking.

THE SHOCK IS INEVITABLE

Thomas rolls over the car hood and tumbles on the road. Angela rushes out in the street and runs to him.

ANGELA

(worried) Thomas!!

Panting, Thomas tries to stand up, helped by Angela.

THOMAS She was there.

He indicates the place where Charli just was.

THOMAS Help me.

The CAR DRIVER steps out of her car.

CAR DRIVER

Are you okay?

Thomas just nods.

CAR DRIVER Sure?

But Thomas is walking away, limping, along with Angela.

ANGELA

Are you really sure?

THOMAS I'm fine.

ANGELA

I mean, are you really sure it was her?

THOMAS

Definitely. I know now it wasn't just a fantasy.

They reach the street corner. Charli and JoDee have disappeared. Thomas turns back.

THOMAS The guy--

ANGELA What guy?

THOMAS

The guy who was yelling at her. Her husband.

He turns back but Scott is now nowhere to be seen.

ANGELA

Are you certain of what you saw?

THOMAS

Yes. I can even feel her presence, smell her perfume.

Angela looks suddenly annoyed. Thomas notices it.

THOMAS

What's that face?

Angela grins a smile.

ANGELA Nothing.

She notices his arm is bleeding.

ANGELA

Let's go back to the hotel.

FADE TO:

INT. HOLIDAY INN - ROOM - DAY

Thomas is seated on the bed, half naked. He has a deep scrape on his arm. Angela is seated by him, cleaning the wound with a wet towel. With delicate and sensual moves, she gently rubs his skin.

Thomas stares at her. She looks up to him.

They eyes meet. Imperceptibly, their faces get closer, and closer.

They are about to kiss, when Thomas draws a grin and moans.

Angela holds her move.

ANGELA Sorry.

Wordless, Thomas gets up, enters the bathroom, and closes the door.

INT. HOLIDAY INN - ROOM - BATHROOM - DAY

Thomas leans over the sink and looks at his own reflection in the mirror. He looks lost.

INT. HOLIDAY INN - ROOM - DAY

CLOSE-UP ON ANGELA'S FACE

A mix of sadness and anger can be read in her eyes.

INT. LOU'S RESIDENCE - LIVING ROOM - DAY

Charli and JoDee enter Lou's residence. Charli looks at the verge of the nervous breakdown. JoDee helps her to sit down.

JODEE

Stay still. I get you something to drink.

She pours a glass of whisky and hands it to Charli.

CHARLI What's that?

JODEE

(nodding)

Drink it up. You'll feel better, believe me. I practiced.

Charli lifts the glass to her lips and frowns.

CHARLI Whisky?

She drinks it up and coughs in front of JoDee's amazed look.

CHARLI More.

JoDee pours her another glass. Charli is about to drink when Lou enters, happy like a little girl.

LOU

(overexcited)

Okay girls. We're having a party here tonight! I invited everyone I know. It's gonna be huge! Are you in?

Charli raises her glass.

CHARLI I'm in!

She drinks bottom up.

FADE TO BLACK:

INT. HOLIDAY INN - ROOM - DAY

Thomas steps out of the bathroom, dressed up, and opens the room door. Angela hasn't moved.

THOMAS I'm off.

ANGELA

Where are you going?

THOMAS

(bitterly)

Listen, Angela. I don't need a chaperon anymore.

ANGELA Remember. You're under my responsibility.

THOMAS

I don't really think you'll appreciate where I'm going.

ANGELA Where to?

THOMAS Hanging bars.

He steps out.

INT. HOLIDAY INN - LIFT - DAY

Thomas and Angela stand in the hotel lift.

ANGELA

Are you going to get drunk?

THOMAS

Would you stop preaching me? I'm just gonna look after Charli's husband. I'm sure he must hang the bars around the street where we were.

Angela smiles.

THOMAS

I can think by myself. Can't I?

INT. BAR #1 - DAY

A loud Country music plays.

Thomas, followed by Angela, enters a bar. He scans the place but can not see Scott.

INT. BAR #2 - DUSK

Same situation in another bar. The place is rather ill-famed, full of Hell's Angels. But no trace of Scott.

INT. BAR #3 - DUSK

A bar with a Jamaican atmosphere.

Still no trace of Scott.

EXT. AMARILLO STREETS - NIGHT

Thomas and Angela enter a Country music cafe.

INT. COUNTRY MUSIC CAFE - NIGHT

LOUD COUNTRY MUSIC

Thomas and Angela enter the cafe. Once again, Thomas scans the place. Scott is nowhere to be seen.

ANGELA

Would you buy me a drink? I never tasted beer.

Quite surprised, Thomas smiles. He steps to the counter.

Before following him, Angela raises her eyes to the ceiling.

ANGELA

(sighing)

I perfectly know what I'm doing.

Okay?

She joins Thomas at the counter who has just ordered two beers. By them, an OLD WINO, wearing a large Stetson hat, is flopped on the counter, staring at his full glass by a bottle as if he was admiring the Madonna.

Then, he raises his glass.

OLD WINO

To Zsa Zsa Gabor. My first and only love.

He drinks up and fills his glass again.

As soon as the BARTENDER puts the two glasses of beer on the counter, Angela grabs hers and looks at Thomas.

ANGELA

Cheers. That's what you usually say?

She puts her glass at her lips and pretends to drink. Thomas drinks up.

LIKE BY MAGIC, ANGELA'S BEER DISAPPEARS IN HER GLASS

The old wino is about to drink when he sees Angela's glass. He stays bug-eyes. He drinks his glass bottom up.

After a few gulps, Thomas puts his glass on the counter and realizes Angela's empty.

ANGELA I love that.

THOMAS

(puzzled) You--?

She nods, smiling.

By them, the old wino does not stop to stare at them and watches every move.

ANGELA Ready for round two?

Astound, Thomas orders two more beers. Angela nods to Thomas' glass.

ANGELA (cont'd)

(encouraging Thomas) Come on.

Thomas smiles and drinks his glass bottom up. He has foam on his lips. Angela gently wipes it up with her thumb. They both take their second glass and clink them.

ANGELA Cheers.

THOMAS Bottom up?

ANGELA

(happily) Okay.

While Thomas drinks, Angela's glass is again magically emptied. This time it is Thomas' turn to wipe the foam up Angela's lips.

Suddenly, Thomas freezes. He sees Scott who steps out from the toilets and sits to a table where he had left his drink. Thomas steps directly to him.

Angela is about to follow him when she is stopped by the old wino.

OLD WINO

Can't you fill up my bottle like you empty your glass?

Angela smiles at him and shakes her head, sorry. Then, she joins Thomas.

SCOTT

(raising his eyes to them) Well, well, look who's here. My dear FBI pair. Come on, have a

drink with me, and let's celebrate   my next divorce.

Between his fingers, Charli's wedding ring. Thomas sits at the table. Angela stays up.

THOMAS Where is she?

SCOTT

(frowning) Who are you people?

ANGELA

(sitting) We're with the FBI.

Struck by Angela's reply, Thomas however decides to play her game. He pretends to look for something.

THOMAS

(badly lying)

I left my badge at the hotel.

SCOTT

(chuckling)

FBI. I knew it. (sigh)

What has she done?

THOMAS

We can't tell, but we need to find her.

Scott drinks a gulp.

SCOTT

(as to himself)

I found my own Hell here. (showing around)

Always hate that damned music. I've even learned that Country song to have her back. For nothing. (chuckling)

I hate everything.

He empties his glass and stares at Thomas who turns to the bartender and beckons him to bring Scott another beer.

SCOTT

I always thought she was happy. Never had to work. I even took a second job. I made her laugh. But she wanted a baby. A baby. Who need a baby nowadays? What fun is it to walk in a shitty diaper in the middle of the night?

The bartender brings Scott another glass and steps back.

SCOTT

I tried my best. I would never understand why she does all this to me.

ANGELA Did you ask her?

SCOTT What would you ask to a brick wall?

To the iceberg Queen?

ANGELA She should have some good reasons.

SCOTT

Who know what could happen in a woman's mind?

ANGELA Her husband?

SCOTT

(chuckling) Touché.

He drinks his beer.

THOMAS

So, where is she now?

Scott digs out into his pocket and takes a fold paper he hands to Thomas.

SCOTT

I don't give a damn anymore.

Thomas unfolds the paper and reads it. He gets up. Angela stares at Scott with goodness.

ANGELA

You'll find someone else. She'll be good to you.

SCOTT Go to Hell.

Angela sadly smiles and follows Thomas on his way out. Scott stares at them on their way out.

EXT. AMARILLO STREET - NIGHT

Thomas walks down a street, inflexible. Angela can hardly follows him.

ANGELA

Are you quite sure of your choice?

Don't you be afraid? Life's full of   surprises.

Thomas stops and turns to her.

THOMAS What do you mean?

ANGELA

You're going to meet her. Good. But if things won't happen like you wish? If she does not want you or doesn't recognize you?

THOMAS

(firmly) We're meant to each other.

ANGELA

Don't be childish Thomas. I would have warned you.

THOMAS

I want to believe in miracles today.

Thomas resumes walking.

FADE TO:

INT. LOU'S RESIDENCE - LIVING ROOM - NIGHT

The Two Angels

LOUD COUNTRY MUSIC

The wild party is on. An incredible crowd is gathered in Lou's living room. Extravagant people, couples, cowboys, people dancing.

Lou wends her way through the dancing couples, carrying empty glasses, toward a supper table where Charli and JoDee are chatting.

LOU

(shouting)

Come on, girls. Move your fat! Be sexy!!

JODEE

(shouting)

We know no one here.

Lou beckons JoDee to wait. She turns to the DJ and signs him to stop the music.

MUSIC STOPS

LOU

(talking loud)

Your attention please! I have to tell you I have by my side two lovely single young women who long for a prince charming! It's up to you gentlemen!! The race is on!!

Charli and JoDee are blushing.

MUSIC RESUMES About ten men rush to the two young women.

LATER

The Two Angels

Charli and JoDee happily talk with two men (BRAD and KENNY), a glass in hand.

INT. LOU'S RESIDENCE - LOBBY - NIGHT

The bell rings at the front door. Lou, who walks by, a glass in hand, opens the door. Thomas and Angela appear on the doorstep.

LOU

Hi. Can I help you?

THOMAS

(hesitating)

I'm looking for Charli.

LOU

Charli? Yeah, of course. She's here. Come in please.

Thomas and Angela step in.

LOU

Had she invited you?

THOMAS

(hesitating)

Not exactly, but we traveled a long way to see her.

LOU

Just a minute. I'm gonna get her for you.

She gives Thomas her glass and leaves them for the living room. Thomas looks very nervous, not knowing what to do with the glass. He rearranges his fringe and breathes deeply.

INT. LOU'S RESIDENCE - LIVING ROOM - NIGHT

Lou makes her way through the party to Charli. She leans over her ear.

LOU

(shouting)

There's someone for you at the door.

CHARLI

(to JoDee) Scott.

LOU

(shouting)

I don't know. A young man and a woman. They said they came a long way to see you.

Charli frowns and hesitates.

JODEE

(to Charli)

I'm coming with you.

They slip through the dancers to the lobby.

INT. LOU'S RESIDENCE - LOBBY - NIGHT

Thomas stands stiff. Charli enters the lobby and stops. She frowns as if she were trying to remember if she knows the man standing before her. Thomas makes one step to her and reaches out his hand.

THOMAS

Hi Charli, I am Thomas Hanson.

CHARLI

(confused)

Do-- Do I know you?

THOMAS

We-- met in a special place, a few days ago. Don't you remind me?

CHARLI

A few days ago? I would remember. (beat)

Somehow--

(shaking her head)

No, sorry Sir. I don't know you. No.

She is about to step back.

THOMAS

We met up there. In Heaven. We were both dead.

Frozen, Charli turns back to him with fearful eyes.

CHARLI

No! That's impossible! You're lying! I don't know you! Leave me alone! Okay?!

She turns her back to him and rushes to the living room, leaving JoDee dumbfounded.

THOMAS

(calling) Charli!

JODEE

(to Thomas)

Do not insist. She said she does not know you.

THOMAS

Are you JoDee? Just tell her I'm telling the truth. I really have to talk to her.

As JoDee leads them back on the doorstep, Thomas turns to her.

THOMAS

If she'll ever remember me, tell her I'm staying at the Holiday Inn.

Thomas Hanson.

Thomas and Angela step out. JoDee closes the door on Thomas' nose.

EXT. LOU'S RESIDENCE - NIGHT(MORE)

Aghast, Thomas walks down the Lou's residence lane to the gate. Angela stands two steps behind him.

ANGELA

You refused to listen to me. Somehow, I warned you. I wanted to spare you pain and sadness, but you're too stubborn, blinded by what you call love!

THOMAS

(desperate)

Want me telling you were right?! Okay, you were right! From the start. Okay?!

THOMAS(cont'd)

I'm only human after all! And you are a superior being! An angel! Big deal!

ANGELA

    Don't be mad at me.

EXT. LOU'S RESIDENCE - STREET - NIGHT They reach the street.

THOMAS

But I want you to explain one thing. Why she has no recollection of me? Why do I remember everything and not her?!

ANGELA

You didn't step through the HBW.

Thomas stops.

THOMAS The what?!

ANGELA

What we call the Heaven Brain Wash. Everyone who's coming back to life goes through this and gets all his souvenirs from above annihilated.

You broke the protocol, Thomas. That's why.

THOMAS

Then, she will never remember me?

The Two Angels

ANGELA She can't. That's one of the conditions for coming back.

(THOMASMORE)

(increasingly furious) You knew it from the start! Why did you help me then all the way? To be sure I would come back with you afterwards? Yeah! A desperate man is easier to handle, isn't it? (with spite)

You're not better that any human being. If being an angel means to manipulate people, to hurt, to cheat or to lie, I'm not urging to go back up and be like you! Listen. I've still have four days ahead. And I'll do my best to prove her who I am! Whatever you'd do! (beat)

THOMAS(cont'd)

Did I respond enough for you this time?!

He keeps walking and stops.

THOMAS

And before you ask me, I go back to the hotel!

He is already gone and leaves Angela standing there.

LOU'S RESIDENCE - BATHROOM - NIGHT

Charli is leaned over the sink, refreshing her face with cold water. JoDee enters the bathroom.

JODEE

Don't you really know who's that guy?

CHARLI

I don't. Scott surely sent him. No one knows what's happened to me besides him and you. It's really cruel.

JoDee hesitates for a short while.

JODEE

You forgot someone. The guy you met up there.

(beat)

Listen. Did you tell Scott about it? You said you didn't. So, how could he would send this guy to tell this tale?

Charli thinks for a while.

CHARLI

Remember what we're agreed. If I met him in Heaven, he'd surely be dead.

JODEE

You did come back, didn't you? Why not him?

CHARLI

But why does he seem to recall everything and not me?

JODEE

Hey, I don't have all the answers!

I'm just trying to help you. (beat)

So, what are you gonna do?

Charli turns the water off and towels off.

CHARLI

(firmly)

The Two Angels

Forget all about this and get a real life. Remember?

INT. LOU'S RESIDENCE - LIVING ROOM - NIGHT

The party is still on. Charli closely dances, having fun, with Brad. By the buffet, JoDee chats with Kenny, she keeps an eye on Charli. CLOSE-UP ON THE WINDOWPANE

Outside, Angela stares at Charli, thoughtful.

FADE TO BLACK:

INT. HOLIDAY INN - ROOM - NIGHT

Thomas is laid on the bed, hands under his head. He fixes the ceiling. Angela enters the room.

ANGELA

(sweet)

Thomas, I'm sincerely sorry. (beat)

I mean it. I realized that for me it was only a mission, but, for you, it might be something that will change your whole life.

She gently sits on the bed by him.

ANGELA

It's wasn't a lie when I told you I wanted to protect you. Human beings are so fragile, so emotive. Especially you. Thomas looks at her.

ANGELA

Maybe you were right when you told me I was jealous. You touched me,

Thomas.

The Two Angels

(beat)

May I lay down by you?

Thomas nods. She lays down by him, her head on his arm, her hair almost touching his lips.

ANGELA

I felt by you something I haven't feel for anyone for so many years. I couldn't help it. You must know that it's perfectly forbidden for us, angels, to fall in love with human beings, to burn our wings. The ones who did became what we call fallen angels. That's why I fought this feeling inside, but the more the deadline gets close, the more I'm

    scared. Scared to lose you up there.

Thomas can smell her hair. He closes his eyes and breathes in.

ANGELA

Something deep inside of me tells me that you're not totally insensible. I can almost hear your heartbeat banging on your chest. Am I wrong, Thomas?

She turns her head to him. Their faces are very close. Angela puts her hand on Thomas' cheek and forces him to look at her. Their lips are getting closer.

ANGELA

(whispering)

I'll make you forget all this, Thomas. You will know no more troubles. No more pain.

The Two Angels

Their lips are almost touching.

Closer.

CLOSER

ANGELA No more tears.

She caresses his face. Thomas closes his eyes again. Her lips touch and they kiss.

A long and languorous kiss. Angela rolls on Thomas and they embrace.

Angela starts to undress Thomas who lets her do.

FADE TO BLACK:

INT. HOLIDAY INN - ROOM - DAY

Thomas is awaken by a sunray. Angela is laid by him, on her elbow, staring at him. As he turns by her, she kisses him on the cheek.

ANGELA Hi, Thomas.

THOMAS (feeling well) 'morning.

ANGELA

Did you sleep well?

THOMAS

(in a sigh) Like an angel.

He gets closer to her and about to kiss her but Angela avoids his kiss and gets up.

ANGELA

Thank you for that night.

THOMAS

Thank you to you. No one made love to me like you did last night. It was-- divine. (sighs)

I'm starving.

INT. LOU'S RESIDENCE - KITCHEN - DAY

JoDee has a copious breakfast in the kitchen. Charli enters, woozy, half-asleep, holding her forefront.

CHARLI 'morning.

JODEE

Already up? You really had your fun last night.

CHARLI

I guess.

(beat)

I have a date tonight. With Brad. Did you notice how cute was his round little ass?

JODEE

I particularly noticed you drank more than you could bear.

Charli starts to fix her breakfast.

CHARLI

Hell with my ex dull life. (yawning)

I need some coffee.

JODEE

And what about that guy of last night, Thomas? He looked so sincere to me.

CHARLI

Told you he was just a stupid and cruel schizo. No one can come back from the dead.

JODEE

But-- Everything you told me. Your dream? The face-- lost in the crowd?

CHARLI

It was an unclear memory. Just a dream. You can't build a life on a dream, can you?

JoDee stays silent for a short while, staring at Charli. She sighs.

JODEE

Charli. Would you do me a favor? I never asked you anything. Talk with that guy. Why don't you invite him at the concert on New Year's Eve?

Charli stares at her, confused.

JODEE

Sorry, I forgot to tell you. We're all invited to a Country music gig on Saturday night. Invite him and spend the evening with him. You will see if he's a schizo or not. You have nothing to lose. Then, you'll forget him if you want.

CHARLI

I don't even know where to find him?

The Two Angels

JODEE

He stays at the Holiday Inn.

CHARLI

(thinking) I don't know.

JODEE

(with a smile)

Oh, yes. I almost forgot your motto.

(beat) Seriously. Think about yourself.

Think about what you told me about what you felt.

CHARLI Holiday Inn?

JODEE

(nodding) His name is Thomas Hanson.

CHARLI Yeah. I remember that.

(beat) Got an aspirin?

FADE TO:

EXT. HOLIDAY INN - TERRACE - DAY

Angela is in on her phone on the hotel terrace, walking around. She wears sunglasses.

ANGELA

(on the phone)

He still has three days left but he won't succeed now. As I expected, she does not have any reminiscence of him and he is close now to come back with me. (beat)

The Two Angels

What about me? I'm perfectly fine. I'm playing his game to better bring his back. That's all. I can't really see--
(MORE)

(beat)

How can you say I changed? Maybe I'm enjoying my stay here more than

I thought. (beat)

Yes. Why not? Who wouldn't? I'm an angel but not a saint. If really you don't trust me, go ahead, tell me straightly. Did I ever deceived you in the past? I've been working for you for more than eight hundred and fifty years and how many complaints did you have about me? Huh? Tell me! (beat)

I lied to him and what? Let's rather say, I sinned by omission.

ANGELA(cont'd)

I had to. It was part of my plan.

Anyway, it's not my fault if he escaped.

(beat)

I don't mind to be downgraded to second-class angel, I'm just doing my job!

She hangs up, furious.

INT. HOLIDAY INN - RESTAURANT - DAY

Angela enters the restaurant where Thomas has a copious breakfast and sits at his table. Thomas stares at her with different eyes.

THOMAS

(worried)

What's wrong with you? You look frenzied.

Angela tries do smile.

ANGELA

I'm alright. Let's say, they urge me above to bring you back.

THOMAS

Did you tell them we were on the way? That I was finally agreed?

ANGELA

Yes. But, they're rather in a hurry. They're afraid you'd change your mind again.

THOMAS

And about the fact we'll stay together?

Angela stares straight in his eyes.

ANGELA

(lying) They agree.

She freezes. She sees Charli who has just entered the restaurant and now scans the room.

As Thomas turns his back to Charli, Angela gets up and places behind him.

ANGELA I feel you tense.

She starts to massage his shoulders. Thomas appreciates and closes his eyes.

CHARLI (O.S.) Do I bother?

Thomas opens his eyes, but Angela keeps on massaging him.

THOMAS

(embarrassed) No!

He manages to escape Angela's massage.

CHARLI

(to Thomas)

I wanted to invite you somewhere, but I realize you have better to do.

Thomas gives Angela a dark look.

THOMAS She's only--

Thomas does not know what to say.

CHARLI

(frowning) Yes?

THOMAS

(stuttering)

She's-- a friend of mine. My best friend. She came to support me and help me to find you.

ANGELA

(falsely)

Oh, yes, of course.

CHARLI

(shaking her head)

Pathetic. I don't know who you are, but if you have made a long way to find me, you may return where you belong.

Upset, she rushes to the restaurant exit. Thomas gets up but Angela grabs his arm and holds him back.

THOMAS

(struggling)

Leave me alone! Don't you see you're playing with my life?

ANGELA

Don't you hear her?

Thomas stares at her.

THOMAS

(realizing) I can't believe it! You're jealous!

ANGELA What are you talking about?

THOMAS You're jealous!

Everybody stares at them in the restaurant.

ANGELA

I'm not! I'm just trying to protect you!

THOMAS

Protect me?! Against what?! Happiness?!

The Two Angels

ANGELA

Remember what we did last night. Does it mean anything to you?

THOMAS What YOU did!

ANGELA

Thomas, you betrayed her.

Thomas turns pale as if he was finally realizing what he did. He sighs, escapes from her grab and sprints to the restaurant entrance where he bumps into JoDee.

THOMAS

(in a flurry)

Where is she? I have to talk to her!

JODEE

Not now. She's too upset. You have to trust me. I'm her closest friend. I'm know her the best.

Thomas sighs and turns to Angela with anger.

THOMAS

    (to JoDee)

Can we talk?

EXT. HOLIDAY INN - TERRACE - DAY Thomas and JoDee stand on the terrace.

JODEE

Tell me straightly. Did Scott send you?

THOMAS Who's Scott?

The Two Angels

JODEE Charli's husband.

(beat) No. You're not.

(sigh) I'm not supposed to talk to you.

Charli would mad at me. But if you really are who I think you are, I hope I can get things settled. You said you met her in Heaven?

THOMAS

Yes. You should think I'm a schizo--

JoDee cannot help smiling.

JODEE

That's what Charli thinks.

Thomas sighs.

THOMAS But this is the truth. (beat)

A few days ago, I committed suicide and--

FADE TO:

LATER

JODEE

Your story is as astonishing as (MORE) Charli's one. She told me she has unclear memories from her coma but one thing she clearly remembers is having tell a man--

THOMAS

(interrupting)

--"thank you". (nodding) Yes.

The Two Angels

JoDee stays dumbfounded.

JODEE

(excited)

So, it's truly you. Wow!

JODEE(cont'd)

(beat)

I think Charli is simply scared about all this. Who wouldn't be?

She happily takes two concert tickets out her pocket.

JODEE

Meet her on New Year's Eve. I'll try to get her prepared.

Thomas takes the two tickets and has a glimpse on them.

THOMAS

Thank you. I'll be there.

JoDee puts her hand on his arm.

JODEE

Thomas, I envy you. You made a long way to find her. That's very-- romantic.

THOMAS

That's my last chance too.

JODEE Good luck then.

She kisses him on the cheek and rapidly steps out of the terrace.

INT. HOLIDAY INN - RECEPTION - DAY

On his way back, Thomas crosses the reception. The receptionist hails him.

RECEPTIONIST Mister Hanson.

Thomas steps to the counter.

THOMAS Yes?

RECEPTIONIST

You forgot this last night at the lounge.

He hands Thomas his scrapbook.

THOMAS

What do you mean last night?

RECEPTIONIST

The waiter picked it up after you left.

THOMAS

(bewildered)

But-- I stayed all night in my--

RECEPTIONIST

He told me you spent the most part of the night drawing and you left around three.

Furious, Thomas takes the scrapbook and pages through.

THOMAS Thank you.

INT. HOLIDAY INN - RESTAURANT - DAY

Angela sees Thomas coming to her. She notices his face.

THOMAS

(firmly)

We have to talk.

FADE TO:

INT. HOLIDAY INN - ROOM - DAY

Thomas lets Angela enters the room and closes the door behind him.

ANGELA

What's wrong Thomas?

THOMAS

(furious)

What the fuck have you done to me this time?!

Angela stares at him ingenuously.

THOMAS

(furious)

Referring the receptionist, I spent most of my last night drawing in the lounge and left this.

He throws the scrapbook on the bed.

THOMAS

What's the trick?

ANGELA

There's no trick, Thomas. We made love, that's all. He should be mistaken.

THOMAS

(shouting)

It's full of drawings I don't remember!

He tries to calm down.

THOMAS

Did you use some kind of awaken dream charm on me?

She is about to speak.

THOMAS

And no cock-and-bull story this time! I warn you!

Angela is stuck.

FLASHBACK - HOLIDAY INN - ROOM - NIGHT

ANGELA (V.O.)

(sweet)

Last night, I tried to seduce you.

Angela is laid by Thomas and turns her head to him. Their faces are very close. Angela puts her hand on Thomas' cheek and forces him to look at her. Their lips are getting closer.

ANGELA

(whispering)

I'll make you forget all this, Thomas. You will know no more troubles. No more pain.

Their lips are almost touching.

The Two Angels

CLOSER

ANGELA No more tears.

She caresses his face.

ANGELA (V.O.) Only, it didn't work.

At the very moment they are going to kiss, Thomas gets up, grabs his scrapbook on the room table, and steps out of the room.

ANGELA (V.O.) You left with your scrapbook and came back early this morning.

END OF THE FLASHBACK:

INT. HOLIDAY INN - ROOM - DAY Angela lowers her eyes.

ANGELA

Yes. You're right. I set up all this.

Thomas stares at her, eyes full of hatred.

ANGELA

Thomas. You're the first man ever who refuses an angel's love.

She reaches her hand out to him but does not dare to touch him.

ANGELA

I never wanted to hurt you. And I realize that your love for her is true. What can I do to make me forgiven? Tell me. I'll do anything. (beat) Anything.

FADE TO BLACK:

INT. CIVIC CENTER - NIGHT

A large and crowded concert hall.

On stage, a band plays Country music. The audience swings and cheers to the music beat in a real frantic atmosphere, sweating and singing.

In the VIP Square, several people listen to the music, drink champagne or dance.

Lou is here, talking with a woman.

Charli holds Brad's arm. She looks glad to be with him. They happily clink their champagne glasses.

JoDee is on her own, looking nervous. She looks as if she was expecting for someone.

As the band stops the music, the audience cheers.

Brad leans over Charli's ear and says something. Charli laughs like a little girl. At her turn, she speaks to his ear and they laugh together, drinking.

Charli cheers to JoDee who answers with a smile and takes a glimpse to her watch, impatient.

Then, JoDee smiles. Thomas has just entered the VIP Square, followed by Angela. She wears her long black coat and her chignon.

On stage, a female Country singer starts a slow song.

Charli is about to dance with Brad when JoDee pats on her shoulder and nods towards Thomas. When she sees him, Charli freezes, angry.

The Two Angels

JoDee beckons her to talk to him. Exasperated, Charli steps to Thomas and leaves Brad by himself.

CHARLI

How do you dare to come here? Who invited you?

Thomas turns his head to JoDee who smiles at them.

CHARLI

What do you want?

THOMAS

Just one dance with you.

CHARLI

Then you'll leave?

THOMAS As you will.

CHARLI

(affirmative)

Then you'll leave.

Thomas nods.

CHARLI

Just one dance? (sigh) Okay.

In front of Angela, JoDee and Brad's amazed look, they embrace and start to dance.

CHARLI

Why do you harass me?

THOMAS

The Two Angels

You don't remember anything, do you?

CHARLI Remember what?

(sarcastic) Being dead or being in Heaven?

THOMAS When we met.

CHARLI No.

THOMAS

Even when you mouthed "thank you" to me?

Charli turns to JoDee, furious.

CHARLI

She told you everything. I'm gonna--

THOMAS

(interrupting) I was there, Charli.

He turns to Angela and simply nods.

Angela simply closes her eyes as if she'd concentrate on them. As if she were waking up from a dream, Charli stares at Thomas with different eyes.

CHARLI

It was you? The man on the escalator?

THOMAS

(smiling) Yes, Charli.

CHARLI

It was so hazy in my head. How did you find me?

THOMAS

The Two Angels

Let's say I had an angel who came down to give me a hand.

He indicates Angela.

THOMAS

It hasn't been that easy, but I finally made it.

CHARLI

(turning to Angela) You mean, she--?

THOMAS

(smiling)

Yes, she is. And she just gave you your memories back.

Suddenly, Charli stiffens. She pushes Thomas back with some kind of fear in her eyes.

CHARLI

No, it can't be! It's impossible! I never--

JoDee stares at them, floored by Charli's reaction.

CHARLI

(to Thomas)

I've never been dead! No, we never met! You're a liar! It was just a dream!

She starts to sob.

CHARLI

(shouting)

GET AWAY FROM ME!!

She races out of the VIP Square. Thomas does not know what to do anymore.

ANGELA Get her, quick!

With no second thought, Thomas pursues her and sprints out of the VIP Square at his turn.

INT. CIVIC CENTER - HALLWAYS - NIGHT

Through the hallways, out of breath, Thomas runs, searching everywhere, but Charli is nowhere to be seen. On his way, he bumped into several people.

Suddenly, at the end of one hallway, he sees her making her way outside.

EXT. CIVIC CENTER - NIGHT It is pouring rain.

Thomas rushes out. As soon as he steps out, he is instantly soaked and he stops. He sees Charli who runs towards the parking lot.

THOMAS

(shouting)

    Charli!!

But the rain thudding covers his voice. Thomas resumes running after her.

EXT. CIVIC CENTER - PARKING LOT - NIGHT

A true hide-and-seek game starts in the parking lot.

Thomas stops, lost, scanning everywhere around.

Charli could be behind any cars.

THOMAS

(shouting) Charli!!

He feels a presence behind him. He turns back and sees Angela.

Though the pouring rain, she is not wet, like she was unreal. She slowly points her finger to a direction and Thomas follows it. Charli is there, running down the road under the rain.

EXT. AMARILLO STREET - NIGHT

Blinded by the rain and out of breath, Charli runs straight ahead. She is still crying, at the edge of the nervous breakdown.

A few feet behind her, Thomas is faster, near to catch her up.

THOMAS

(shouting) Charli!!

EXT. AMARILLO STREET - CROSSROAD - NIGHT

Charli reaches a crossroad and cannot see a car hurling onto her. At the very last moment, Thomas catches her up and manages to grab her back into his arms.

The car drives on, horn blaring at her, and disappears into the rainy night. Sobbing, Charli cuddles up against Thomas and holds him tight.

THOMAS

(out of breath) Are you okay?

Charli catches her breath, trembling.

CHARLI

(panting)

That's the second time you save my life. When we were up there, my heart started to beat again at the moment I saw you. That's why I came back to life.

THOMAS Why did you run away?

CHARLI

I don't know. I was so scared. All this seemed at the same time too crazy and too good to be true.

Thomas hugs her.

THOMAS

I will never let you go now.

She hugs him back.

Thomas turns his head and sees Angela. With a benevolent smile, she slightly waves to him goodbye. Thomas mouths "thank you" and she simply fades out to disappear like a hologram would do.

Thomas hugs Charli tighter and closes his eyes.

FADE OUT:

FADE IN:

INT. APARTMENT - NIGHT

A large apartment with white bright walls. The same Christmas song from opening credits plays.

On a corner is Thomas' large drawing board with a finished comics page.

Close-up on different pictures under frame:

- Thomas and Charli by the Grand Canyon
- Thomas and Charli on a beach with Linda
- Thomas and Charli with Violet and George
- Thomas and Charli on their wedding day
- a printed comics cover signed Thomas Hanson

By the window where the snow falls outside, Thomas and Charli are decorating a huge Christmas tree.

Charli turns her back to us.

Thomas stands on a footstool. He places garlands on the tree, while Charli hangs glass balls.

CHARLI

It would be my first unforgettable Christmas. Is Linda still coming tonight?

THOMAS

Yes, with her new girlfriend. By the way, I forgot to say. Your mom called and is expecting us for New Year's Eve.

Charli turns to take some candy sticks from a hardboard box. She's pregnant.

Thomas steps down and rummages through the box. He takes an angel out and climbs back on the footstool.

Suddenly, Charli puts her hands on her round belly.

THOMAS Are you alright?

CHARLI

Yes. She just kicked me.

She sits down.

CHARLI

Did you finally think about a name for her?

Thomas puts the angel on the top of the tree. He realizes then that the angel has in fact-ANGELA'S FACE

The angel even looks like winking at him.

THOMAS

What do you think of-- Angela?

FADE OUT:

THE END

Country Music songs suggested through the story:

LONESTAR "Winter Wonderland"

GEORGE STRAIT "Love Without End, Amen"

THE JUDDS "Girls With Guitars"

THE JUDDS "Change Of Heart"

EMMYLOU HARRIS "Amarillo" CARRIE UNDERWOOD "Inside Your Heaven" and

ALABAMA "Angels Among

Printed in Great Britain
by Amazon